A BITTER PILL

A Lenny Moss Mystery

By Timothy Sheard

THE REVIEWERS PRAISE LENNY MOSS!

This Won't Hurt A Bit

"Things get off to a macabre start...when a student at a Philadelphia teaching hospital identifies the cadaver she is dissecting in anatomy class as a medical resident she once slept with. Although hospital administrators are relieved when a troublesome laundry worker is charged with the murder, outraged staff members go to their union representative, a scrappy custodian named Lenny Moss, and ask him to find the real killer. Since there's no merit to the case against the laundry worker to begin with, Lenny is just wasting his time. But Sheard, a veteran nurse, makes sure that readers do not waste theirs. His intimate view of Lenny's world is a gentle eyeopener into the way a large institution looks from a workingman's perspective." **New York Times**

Some Cuts Never Heal

"This well-plotted page-turner is guaranteed to scare the bejesus out of anyone anticipating a hospital stay anytime in the near future." **Publishers Weekly**

"Sheard provides…polished prose and elements of warmth and humor. Strongly recommended for most mystery collections." **Library Journal**

"If your pulse quickens for ER on Thursday nights, you'll want a dose of Timothy Sheard's medicine … The well-meaning, hard-working hospital folks will warm your heart, while the cold realities of modern medical care will raise your blood pressure and keep you turning the pages." **Rocky Mountain News**

A Race Against Death

"While most shop stewards do not get involved in murder mysteries, they solve tough problems at work every day. Now they can look up to a fictional role model—Super Steward Lenny Moss." **Public Employee Press** Review

"Timothy Sheard provides a delightful hospital investigative tale that grips readers from the moment that Dr. Singh and his team apply CPR, but fail." **Mysteries Galore**

Slim To None

"Here's a page flipper, a murder mystery set in a hospital where the invisible, everyday workers are the key...Their practical knowledge, solidarity and smarts solve this confusing case that leads us down all sorts of blind paths with lives on the line...a great read, a complicated mystery, good friends, comradeship in hard times, and union workers shown in full humanity. Get it now!"

Earl Silbar, AFSCME 3506, City Colleges of Chicago

No Place To Be Sick

"Does such a wonderful job of showing workers uniting to fight for justice that...unions have used Sheard's books for steward training. Find out if Lenny & his friends win their battle in this roller coaster of a story." **Union Communications**

"There's enough suspense, fear and chills running up and down your spine to make you keep on reading it in one fell swoop. Watch your back if you're alone in the house!" **Pride & A Paycheck**

For Mike Augenbraun
Colleague, mentor and treasured friend

<><><><><>

Well everything in this world, more or less,
Is a rich man's playground.
Shit Jobs, Chris Sheard

A Bitter Pill, Copyright © 2013 by Timothy Sheard. All rights reserved.

This novel is a work of fiction. Names, characters, places and incidents are either the product of the author's imagination, or, if real, used fictitiously.

No part of this book may be reproduced or transmitted in any form or by an electronic or mechanical means, including photocopying, recording or by any information storage and retrieval system, without the express written permission of the publisher, except where permitted by law.

Published by Hard Ball Press.
Information available at: www.hardballpress.com
ISBN: 0-9814518-9-6

Cover art by Patty G. Henderson
www.boulevardphotografica.yolasite.com.

Exterior and interior book design by D. Bass

Library of Congress Cataloging-in-Publication Data
Sheard, Timothy
No Place To Be Sick: A Lenny Moss Mystery/Timothy Sheard
1. Philadelphia (PA) 2. Hospitals. 3. Lenny Moss.

ONE

A bored security guard ran his eyes over the shapely young woman as he handed her a visitor pass and pointed toward the bank of elevators. His eyes were locked on her fetching figure as she was walking away when he heard a stern voice say, "*Excuse me!*" Turning to the newcomer, the guard saw a short, middle aged woman with a frowning, thin-lipped mouth staring at him. The frown looked like a permanent fixture on her sour face. Behind the woman stood a tall, gray haired man in an old fashioned double breasted suit carrying a thick leather briefcase.

"Yes?" said the guard.

"I am Miss Wiggins, from the National Association of Standards for Hospitals. We are here to conduct a survey of your facility. Kindly notify your chief administrator."

The security guard slid off his seat and all but snapped to attention. He knew that the NASH inspection was a critical test of the hospital's quality of care. Failing the inspection would mean Medicare and the private insurance carriers would stop paying for patient services – a death sentence for the hospital.

"Uh, yes, if you'll have a seat I'll call the office and tell them you're here."

Three minutes later a man in a lab coat accompanied by a stout woman in a pants suit hurried into the lobby.

"Good *morning!*" said the man, beaming. "Welcome to James Madison Medical Center. We are *so* happy you've decided to pay us a visit. I am Doctor Roger Slocum, the chief medical officer, and this is Miss Burgess, our director of nursing."

Miss Wiggins introduced herself and her companion, a Mr. Anderson. Dr. Slocum smiled warmly and all but put his arms around the guests as he led them out of the lobby and down the hall to the administrative wing.

"Let me take you to my conference room where you can settle in. No doubt you'll want to review our policy and procedure manuals and hear about our new patient safety initiatives."

Miss Wiggins said, "I have learned from years of surveying hospitals that those documents don't tell the real story, Doctor Slocum. After we put down our coats and establish a base of operations, I'll want a tour of the facility, starting on the top floor and working our way down to the basement. Have your director of engineering meet us here in fifteen minutes."

"Of course. Mi casa es su casa." Slocum hoped to soften the lead inspector's stern demeanor with a little humor, but he could elicit only a wan smile from the gentleman on the survey team.

While the two inspectors were setting up a temporary office in the conference room, Dr. Slocum called his senior managers to his office. Waiting for the chief of engineering and the director of housekeeping to join him, Slocum complained to Miss Burgess. "This is just great. I came to work with a blinding headache and four meetings already on my schedule, and now these NASH people show up."

"Did you take your migraine medication?" asked the nursing director.

Slocum nodded as he tapped his desk with the end of his pen. "It's bad enough I have all these demands from the new administration. Croesus wants a ten percent decrease in our length of stay starting *this quarter*, and they want a fifteen percent increase in billable services. And now I have the damned survey. Christ, if we fail it..."

"Don't get yourself all worked up, Roger. We've been rehearsing for this survey for months. It's going to go smoothly. I'm sure of it."

Slocum frowned and rubbed his temples while the throbbing in his head built to a crescendo.

<><><><><><>

As soon as the survey team finished setting up their base camp, Miss Wiggins and her companion followed Slocum and the other administrators to the elevator. They rode to the seventh floor, where they inspected the wards. At Seven South, Miss Wiggins stepped into a room labeled SOILED UTILITY and sniffed the air. Seeing a commode chair in the corner, she put on a pair of latex gloves and lifted the lid. Pointing with a disgusted look on her face at the feces in the collecting bucket, she demanded that the director of housekeeping explain who was responsible for cleaning the soiled equipment.

"The nurses empty the potty chair and rinse it in the patient room," said the housekeeping director. "When the patient is discharged, our department will sanitize the chair and the collecting bucket, wrap it in a clear plastic bag and store it in the equipment locker."

Miss Burgess added that she would find out which nurse's aide had left the soiled equipment and discipline her sternly. Miss Wiggins frowned and moved on.

Coming to a closed door labeled ELECTRICAL, the surveyor tried to open the door but found it locked.

"We keep the electrical closets locked at all times for patient safety," explained the hospital engineer.

"Open it," said Wiggins.

The engineer selected his master key from a crowded key ring and opened the closet. Inside were banks of switches and bundles of wires. Miss Wiggins pointed at a paper bag on the floor holding an empty fast food container. "*That* is how you attract vermin to your facility."

The embarrassed housekeeping supervisor scooped it up and carried it past her to a trash receptacle

At a patient room, the surveyor noted a sign on the door that read CONTACT ISOLATION. She stopped the nurse coming out of the room. "Tell me nurse, why is your patient on isolation?"

The nurse explained that the patient was admitted with diarrhea and they were testing him for C. diff.

Wiggins spotted a canister of disposable towels. Picking it up, she read the label on the back. "Is this what you use to clean the environment?"

"Yes," said the nurse. "We wipe down the bedside table and such at the start of every shift."

The surveyor held the canister up close to the nurse's eyes so she could see the label. "This product does not kill *spores.* You should be using a sporicidal product for C. diff patients."

Seeing that the nurse was frozen with fear, the housekeeping director explained that they would supply a bleach product as soon as the test results came back positive for C. diff. Thrusting the canister at the nurse, Miss Wiggins walked to the stairs to go down to the next floor.

As he followed the surveyors down the steps, Dr. Slocum looked at Miss Burgess and made an obscene gesture with his hand, to which the nursing director nodded her head in agreement.

The surveyors moved through Six South, a surgical ward, where they found a few containers of milk in the pantry refrigerator past their due date. Coming to the entrance to Six North, Wiggins saw a sign on the closed fire doors reading HARD HAT AREA: RESTRICTED. The hospital engineer explained that the area was undergoing renovation.

"Let me see it."

Opening the double doors, the engineer followed Wiggins into the work area, where patient rooms were under varying stages of reconstruction.

"We're moving to all single rooms," Slocum said. "It's part of our patient safety initiative related to reducing hospital acquired infections."

"Your reported rates are meaningless, facilities always under report their infections," she said.

They came upon a locked door with no signage to indicate the room's function.

"What's in here?" asked Wiggins.

All the hospital managers looked blank. "A storeroom, maybe?" said the housekeeping supervisor.

Wiggins frowned. "Open it."

The chief of engineering took out his master key and and put it in the lock. At first the lock resisted his efforts, but after fiddling with the key he managed to turn it and unlock the door.

The opened door revealed a room in darkness. The engineer flicked on the light, then stood aside to allow Miss Wiggins to enter. The surveyor stepped into the room, stopped and gasped.

"What in the name of god..."

She lurched backward, bumping into the hospital engineer. Taller than she, he could see over her head a body hanging from a pipe in the open ceiling. A thin rope around the dead man's neck held his feet several inches above the floor. His tongue protruded in an obscene manner from between clenched teeth, and his pants were stained wet where he'd emptied his bladder.

Miss Wiggins turned and hurried out of the room, her face drawn and pale. Her companion turned to the chief medical officer and said, "Dr. Slocum. What is that dead man doing in the room?"

Slocum stepped inside, followed by Miss Burgess. He looked into the face of the dead man and trembled. As a physician he'd pronounced many a patient dead. But he had never come upon someone who had taken his own life, and in such a grotesque manner. He told the housekeeping supervisor to call a code. "Maybe we can revive him. We need to cut him down."

Slocum grabbed the dead man around the hips and lifted while the chief engineer cut the rope with a pocket knife. Concerned the stricken man could be harboring a communicable disease, the physician instructed Miss Burgess to perform the mouth-to-mouth resuscitation while he pressed on the chest.

The code team reached the room within minutes and took over efforts to revive the victim. They ripped open his shirt to apply

EKG leads and pulled his pants off in order to insert a large bore IV catheter in the groin. Officer Jones, a big, beefy security guard, took possession of the dead man's shoes and pants as the team attempted to stimulate the heart and restore its rhythm.

Looking over the failing efforts of the code team, Miss Burgess leaned in close to Dr. Slocum and muttered, "And you thought *you* were having a bad day."

TWO

He was a man of unremarkable appearance. Wearing the blue work clothes, black, steel tipped shoes and worn leather gloves of the housekeeping department, Lenny Moss drew little attention as he guided the buffing machine over the old cracked marble floor. Not very tall, with pale skin that never seemed to tan in the summer and a bald spot at the back of his head, he blended into a crowd like an anonymous extra in a movie.

Although it was no easy task keeping a shine on a surface constantly tracked by dirty stretcher wheels, spilled blood tubes and the occasional burst of vomit, Lenny found working the buffing machine relaxing. He often described it as his 'Zen' time. The back and forth arc of the buffer, the hum of the machine and the repetition of the motion allowed his mind to drift. He could think about his life, or nothing at all, the hum of the machine providing the sound track to his reverie.

Seeing Mimi, one of the Seven South nurses, coming toward him with a worried look on her face, he switched off the machine and let the buffer come to rest.

"Hey, Mimi," he said. "Problem?"

"I'm sorry to bother you, Lenny. Really I am. But could you possibly help me with Mrs. Mudge?"

Lenny arched a single black eyebrow. "What's the old battle-ax complaining about this time?"

"It's her dentures. They're missing, and she's driving me *nuts*. She says she'll have me fired if I don't find them by the time they serve lunch, which is, like, in three hours."

"Well did she go for a test or something this morning?"

"No, she hasn't gone for any tests in two days, and she had her dentures this morning for breakfast. It's *crazy*. I can't imagine what happened to them."

"What makes you think *I* can find them if you already looked?"

Mimi put her hands on her hips and wagged her head side to side. "Don't give me that false modesty crap, Lenny, you're a famous detective. Everybody *knows* you solve problems. If anyone can find the damned dentures, you can."

Parking the buffing machine along the wall and unplugging it for safety sake, Lenny followed the nurse down the corridor to the room. As they entered, Mrs. Mudge sat up in bed and pointed an accusing finger at Mimi.

"You better find my dentures young lady or you can kiss your nursing license good-bye. You'll be lucky to get a job working in a day care center when I'm through with you!"

Mudge's roommate, a pale, elderly woman with thinning white hair, smiled a big toothy grin as Lenny and Mimi passed her bed to reach Mrs. Mudge. "How nice you came to see me, Robert," said the room mate as they passed. "How was your day at the office?"

Mimi whispered to Lenny that Mrs. Headley was confused. "She's got dementia. She thinks every man who comes in the room is her husband and I'm her daughter. And I'm black!"

"That *is* confused," said Lenny, waving at Mrs. Headly. He stood between the two beds looking around. There on Mrs. Mudge's bedside cabinet was her denture cup, the lid off and obviously empty. He went through her bedside cabinet, removing the basin for washing and the toilet items. He pulled the cabinet away from the wall and looked behind it. Then he got down on hands and knees and looked underneath the cabinet and beneath the bed.

No dentures.

"Hmmm. Would you mind sitting in a chair a moment while I look in the bed?"

Grumbling, Mrs. Mudge put her feet over the bed and allowed Mimi to help her stand and transfer to the reclining chair.

Lenny carefully pulled off each piece of linen, including the pillow case, and inspected it. No dentures there. He lifted the mattress and looked beneath it. Nothing.

After carefully remaking the bed, Lenny went to the narrow closet and inspected the contents. Again, he came up empty. A search of the tiny bathroom likewise was equally fruitless.

Lenny's last hope was the roommate's furniture. Mrs. Headly's denture cup was on her bedside cabinet. Lifting the lid, he saw a pair of old, stained dentures soaking in mouth wash, an old nursing trick to make them smell good.

He rummaged inside the bedside cabinet and under the bed with no luck. He even looked beneath the confused woman's pillow. Nothing there.

Puzzled, Lenny stood in the middle of the room and looked it over. The dentures had to be somewhere. But where?

Glancing at Mrs. Headley, who again smiled brightly at him, Lenny broke out in a huge grin himself. Gesturing to Mimi to come closer, he pulled the lid off the confused woman's denture cup and pointed at the set of old stained teeth. Then he said to the demented woman, "Smile for me, ma'am."

The old woman smiled her bright, toothy grin.

"Found the missing dentures," said Lenny.

Mrs. Mudge let out a howl that echoed down the corridor. "You *idiots*! I can never use those dentures again! I'll have your job, nurse, do you hear me?"

Mimi offered to take the dentures from Mrs. Headley's mouth and send them to Central Sterile Supply to have them sterilized, but the angry woman would not be mollified. Giving up trying to placate her, Mimi followed Lenny out into the hall, where they both broke into uncontrollable laughter.

"Did you see the look on Mrs. Mudge's face?" said Mimi. "It was almost worth the trouble I'm gonna be in." Lenny agreed, it was priceless.

As they reached the nursing station, Mimi asked Lenny what was going to happen under the new owners. "There are so many rumors floating around since Croesus took us over. Like they're gonna replace most of us nurses with techs and P-A's. *Crazy* stuff.

Even the doctors are scared."

Lenny admitted he didn't know what was coming, only that it would be bad for all of them. Especially the patients.

He had just switched on the buffer and was trying to get back into his Zen state of mind when he spied his friend Moose Maddox coming toward him with an angry look on his face. Moose was a big man, with powerful arms and huge hands that in his youth had worn boxing gloves.

"Yo, Lenny! You hear about Louie?"

"No, I haven't heard anything. Don't tell me that bozo's got himself in trouble for selling weed again?"

"That ain't it. He's dead. The man is stone cold dead!"

"What? What the hell happened? Was it a heart attack or something?"

"No, man, it wasn't nothin' like that. He hung his self. They found the body this morning inspecting six north. You know, where it's under construction."

Lenny switched off the buffer and stood still a moment, his gloved hands on the handle, trying to grasp what happened. Of all the guys, he never would have predicted Louie taking his own life.

"What you think?" said Moose. "Think he was in trouble with his dealer? Couldn't pay the weight?"

"Maybe. That Roland Weekes is a bad mother. He doesn't play if you short him." Lenny considered the possibilities. "I don't think he was in trouble at work. At least no more than usual." Lenny felt a surge of sadness come over him. And regret. "Jesus H. Christ, that must be what his message to me was all about." Asked what it was, Lenny explained that when he listened to his voice messages this morning he heard a message Louie had left on his cell phone the night before.

"You didn't pick up when he called?" asked Moose.

"No. Ever since Carlton called me at midnight last year from the park I turn my cell off after eight o'clock. Otherwise I'd never get any rest. It wasn't much of a message, though. He just said

'Lenny, it's me, Louie. I'm getting out. Call me.'"

"That's all he said?"

"That's it. He was getting out. Shit. I wish to hell I heard the message and called him back."

Moose poked Lenny in the chest. "Don't beat yourself up, it wasn't your fault. You can't be taking calls at all hours of the day and night."

"I know, but -"

"You can't! Ain't nothin' more to say about it." Moose promised to call Lenny if he heard any more news and hurried off.

Lenny switched on the buffer and finished polishing the floors, troubled by the unexpected death of a co-worker. Why did Louie do it? Could Lenny have read the signs and intervened before the man made the ultimate choice? Well, there was not much to do now except begin taking up a collection for his widow and be sure the benefits office paid out the life insurance without a lot of bullshit delay.

He found a grain of relief knowing at least there was no murder for him to investigate. Nobody was going to ask him to uncover the *real* killer in order to free an innocent worker charged with the crime.

Small comfort in a world where the cannibals ruled the hospital. And the world.

THREE

Miss Burgess sniffed the freshly brewed coffee that Dr. Slocum's secretary had prepared for him, a fragrant, exotic blend from Hawaii. Burgess suspected that Slocum chose the fragrant blend to conceal the smell of the whiskey he put in it.

"Is the inspection called off?" she asked.

"Only for today. Miss Wiggins needs the rest of the day to settle her nerves."

"More like load up on gin and tonics," said the nursing director. "If ever I saw an alcoholic dying for a drink, it was her."

"The gentleman with her was quite philosophical about the whole thing. I think he may even cut us a little slack for the survey. I mean, it's obvious the employee's death has nothing to do with the operation of the hospital."

"I'm sure you're right. I'll tell my head nurses to keep everybody on their toes and be ready in the morning to face the survey." She watched him drain his cup, noting the rapid improvement in his disposition. "The migraine gone?"

"Are you kidding? I've been summoned to the President's office. Doctor Reichart wants a full explanation of the dead guy on the ward. He's worried about the PR fallout."

"What are you going to tell him?"

"Joe West has already emailed me the story. He says the man was a drug dealer and a chronic troublemaker who was perpetually on suspension. He obviously couldn't cope with the stress and strain of the criminal life."

Slocum pulled on his lab coat, then stood still while Burgess adjusted the collar so it was neat and symmetrical. He got an unwelcome whiff of her perfume. Lilac. "Well. once more into the breach," he said and stepped out of the office.

<><><><><><>

Doctor Lasser from the Medical Examiner's office stood in the room under construction looking down at the body on the floor and shaking his head. He turned back to face Joe West, chief of hospital security. "You would think the professionals in a *hospital* would know better than to move the body and interfere with the scene of death."

"The doctors thought they might be able to bring him back," said West. West was dressed in his customary navy blue double-breasted suit, white shirt and handcuffs dangling from the belt. The workers often joked that West's idea of a romantic gift was leather restraints and a neck chain.

"The man died *last night!* He was *stone cold* when they discovered the body," said Lasser, noting the core temperature of the body. "You're saying it wasn't obvious to a *doctor* he'd been dead for hours?"

"I guess the sight shook them up. It's not like a heart attack or something they know."

Dr. Lasser began with a visual inspection of the body, while his assistant Harvey took several photographs. Lasser examined the abrasions on the neck made by the rope. They were deep and purple; definitely made before death. The angle of the bruising looked consistent with a hanging, as opposed to a manual strangulation by a person or persons unknown. Still, he wouldn't be able to make a firm determination until conducting the autopsy.

The shirt had been ripped open, revealing post-mortem bruising of the chest from the CPR. He hoped that hadn't broken a rib in their efforts. Well, the man was fairly young, so the bones shouldn't be too brittle.

After the requisite photos were taken, he helped his assistant stuff the corpse in the body bag, noting, as he had on more than one occasion, that doing so was not unlike packing for a trip, though in these cases it was always one way.

"I don't suppose you found a note on him?" said Lasser.

Joe West shook his head, his cold, shark eyes betraying no emotion.

His assistant scooped up the plastic bag with the dead man's clothing and personal items and pushed the stretcher out the door.

<><><><><><>

Dr. Slocum popped a breath mint into his mouth and entered the office of Robert Reichart, the hospital President and enforcer for the new regime. He found Reichart seated at a wide desk, leaning back in the biggest leather chair Slocum had ever seen, and barking orders into the phone. On the wall behind him was a picture of General George Patton, the World War II American war hero, dressed in a general's uniform. Slocum had learned that Reichart was not only ex-military - a major at that - but also a huge admirer of General Patton. It explained why the President often spoke of management's mission as a military campaign.

"Take a seat," Reichart said, hanging up the phone and jotting a few cryptic words on a legal sized pad. The notes seemed to be in some curious kind of short hand. *Did he write notes in code?*

"What sort of fallout can I expect from the incident today on six north? Will it prejudice the surveyors?"

"I don't see why it should," said Slocum. "An employee committing suicide is not related to any patient care issues. I mean, if it had been a *patient* who hung himself, maybe they would fault our psych evaluation. We evaluate every patient for suicidal thoughts when they first come in."

"I've seen the entry in the charts, it's a standard form the nurse checks off. It's bullshit. Doesn't protect us at all from liability."

Dr. Slocum was about to defend the hospital's admissions process when Reichart raised a hand and silenced him. "I called you down to go over the roll out this afternoon of the new diagnostic program one last time. You have reviewed the program thoroughly?"

"Yes. I was up quite late last night, actually, looking it over. I have to admit, if we had the program last year it would have pumped up the bottom line enormously."

"Never mind last year, tell me how your physicians are going to react."

"Well, I should think most of them will welcome it. After all, it provides them with up to the minute, real time information about their patients. And the treatment options are clearly laid out for them. It's a no-brainer."

"Don't kid yourself. Getting them to embrace the program won't be that easy. We've found physicians at other facilities accusing the program of undermining their autonomy. They didn't understand at first, the program was helping them prevent mistakes. Less mistakes means less lawsuits."

"That's always welcome news."

"But the bottom line is, by utilizing the program's diagnostic terminology, they maximize reimbursement rates. That improves our revenue stream, and *that* means more money in their pockets."

"That's what I was going to point out to them. The program protects their license *and* increases their income. Besides, it doesn't *force* them to adopt the computer's treatment recommendations."

"That's what you're going to tell them, and that's what you're going to reinforce every day. Keep hammering away at the idea that they are still in control of the patient's care. In time, they'll get used to following the computer program's algorithm. Then, once they are comfortable with it, we can begin the non-renewal process and begin consolidating departments."

"So it's true. You are going to lay off some of the physicians."

"They won't be needed. With the computerized program, their input is largely superfluous. A senior physician will monitor the patient's progress, of course. But that's largely for medical-legal requirements."

Slocum felt a new wave of pain course through his head as he slowly rose to his feet. "Uh, how many physicians do you expect to let go?"

"We haven't made a determination yet." Reichart eyed Slocum for a few seconds. "Have no illusions, Roger. Your continuing on as Chief Medical Officer hinges on your ability to sell the program."

With Slocum standing frozen in place, Reichart added, "Joe West better be damn sure he has that union out of here in sixty days. Those union thugs are the single biggest threat to this hospital's financial security. We have to break them and throw them in the gutter where they belong."

Reichart opened a file on his desk and began underlining sections of it, indicating the interview was over. Slocum silently turned and left, annoyed at being treated as some sort of servant, but at the same time hopeful that his job was secure, at least for the immediate future. It would take months, maybe a year or more, to bring all the physicians into line on the new program, and god knows how long it will take to get rid of the union. That would keep him in his position. And after that? It was anybody's guess with Croesus running the facility.

He headed for his office and another cup of coffee.

FOUR

With coffee and bagel in his hands, Lenny Moss entered the sewing room and felt an immediate sense of relief, seeing his friends already there. Moose was sitting on a chair backwards, his big hands resting on the back of the chair, holding a cup of coffee and talking to his wife Birdie. Birdie was feeding an old sheet through her ancient sewing machine, repairing a tear.

"I sure wish they'd let me cut these old sheets up and make them into rags," said Birdie. "Soon's I send them upstairs, they gonna tear all over again when the nurse makes the bed."

"They're nickel and diming us to death," said Moose. "The soup they made today was so damn *thin,* it had hardly no taste to it. They gonna call it a *consume* and send it up anyway. Don't make no sense."

As Lenny unfolded a chair and settled in, Birdie asked him what he thought about the new bosses.

"It's gonna be trouble. There will be layoffs, that much is certain. And when our next contract comes up for negotiation they'll try to cut our benefits."

"Cuts and more cuts, that's all they want," said Moose. "We might as well be picking tobacco down Mississippi."

Lenny asked how the collection for Louie's widow was coming. Birdie said she had already collected money from the girls in the laundry and would go to Central Sterile Supply next.

"Who's collecting in dialysis?" asked Moose.

"Abrahm is assigned to the unit where Louie worked, he'll take up the collection there. Regis is going to the labs, Little Mary is going to the wards, I'll hit up admitting and patient relations."

"I'll talk to some of the office secretaries," said Moose "I got a cousin working in patient records."

Lenny suggested they try to get the collection done by the

weekend. He would take the money to Louie's house and give it to Matilda. "I'll check on his life insurance with the benefits office," he added. "Sometimes they drag their feet paying out."

"Sure was a surprise, him goin' out that way," said Moose. "I never would've figured. He must've owed his dealer big time."

"I'm not so sure that's it," said Lenny, washing down a bite of his bagel with coffee. "But I'll see if I can find anything solid about his drug deals. One time I -"

Crack!

Suddenly the door burst open, interrupting Lenny's story, and his housekeeping partner Little Mary came charging into the room. She was a short, thickly built woman with dark skin who could hoist a heavy bag of trash as well as any man and curse a blue streak as long as any sailor.

"*Lenny*! You got t' do something 'bout the new camera at the time clock! I went down my locker to get my medicine and they was putting the fricking thing up!" She thrust a torn piece of paper in Lenny's face.

Lenny took the paper and held it out nearly at arm's length.

"Man, you *have* to get yourself some glasses," Moose told him. "You ain't as young as you think you are."

Ignoring his friend, Lenny read the announcement, which Mary had torn from the wall above the housekeeping time clock. The paper said that a new camera with facial recognition was being installed at the time clock. It would record a picture of the workers as they punched in and out, as well as deter individuals punching in for somebody else.

"You *b'lieve* this shit?" said Mary.

"Those bastards," said Lenny. "They are slick mothers, I have to give it to them."

The memo added that employees would no longer be allowed to punch in more than fifteen minutes prior to starting their shift or fifteen minutes after it ended.

Looking over Lenny's shoulder, Birdie asked why the fifteen

minute limitation.

"They're trying to break an old tradition in housekeeping," said Lenny. "Some of the old timers like to come in a half hour early. Maybe even an hour. They punch in, then they go off and relax. The bosses hate it. They want us to punch in and go directly to our work assignment."

"But they still get the work done. Ain't that what matters?" said Birdie.

"It's all about control," said Lenny. "And intimidation."

"Can't the union do nothin' about it?" asked Mary. "Ain't it a invasion of privacy?"

"No, I don't think so. There's nothing in the contract that says they can't put a security camera anywhere in the hospital, except for the locker room where we change clothes. And the bathrooms, of course."

"It ain't right!" Little Mary said. "It ain't fair!"

Birdie wondered what they will come up with next. Lenny shrugged his shoulders, knowing there would be more shit rolling down on them; attacks he couldn't even imagine. He promised to talk to their regional union organizer, but warned them he didn't think the union could do anything about the new cameras.

As the break time ended, Moose reminded Lenny to take the stairs back to Seven South.

"That's easy for you to say, the kitchen is on this floor."

"Heh, heh." His friend clapped Lenny on the back. "Don't forget we jogging Saturday morning in Fairmont Park."

"I have an appointment with my chiropodist" said Lenny as he entered the stairwell and began to climb. He knew no excuse would keep Moose from picking him up and dragging him to the park. And though the climb to his ward would leave his legs aching, he was secretly relieved that his body had recovered enough from the last horrific injury to let him begin getting back in shape.

Especially with the long fight with the new administration coming down on them.

FIVE

As physicians, students and the research assistants filed into the auditorium, Dr. Slocum stepped to the podium and gave a glowing introduction to the new president, Dr. Reichthart, and James Madison Hospital's new owner, the Croesus Medical Group. Slocum extolled Croesus's legendary efficiency in stabilizing failing health care facilities and setting them down the road to financial health. Pointing at the image of the Croesus Medical Group logo shining brightly on the huge video screen, he promised that their new, breakthrough computer technology would make their work as physicians simpler, more efficient and more profitable for everyone.

A physician in the audience leaned toward his companion and muttered that the giant big LED display the new owners had installed was as big as an ad in Times Square.

"That's Croesus for you," his companion said. "It's a damn Barnum & Bailey show."

Glancing at Reichart, Slocum saw that the president was growing impatient, so he finished by saying, "It is my honor and my privilege to hand the program over to the leader who will take us soaring into the new decade, Dr. Robert Reichart."

To polite but unenthusiastic applause, Reichart stepped to the podium, where he plucked the microphone from its holder, walked to the edge of the stage and gazed into the hushed crowd for a full minute, building suspense.

"Today, James Madison begins a journey into the future. This future will usher in an era of financial stability for the medical center and a time of financial security and prosperity for the physicians who are the heart and soul of this great institution."

He pointed a device at the large screen behind him and advanced a slide. "How, you may ask, will we accomplish this? By embracing the computerized diagnostic and treatment program that provides *you* with critical, real time patient information. C. Ellison Randolph, the founder and CEO of the Croesus Group, developed the Patient Treatment Application, or PTA, specifically to improve patient outcomes. And it will do that again at James Madison."

He looked out at the faces turned up to him and knew he had them in the palm of his hand.

"The program we have brought online today has two, complimentary components. First, the diagnostic program imports patient data in a continuous data stream." He advanced a slide to show the components of the diagnostic program.

"Real time information about the patient's vital signs, lab results, x-ray reports, pathology reports, and medications are sorted, rated as to relevance and compared for efficacy and potential adverse interaction. For example, consider the patient with the early stages of sepsis."

Click.

The vital signs and other information of a case report appeared.

"When this patient's blood pressure, heart rate, white blood cell count and lactate level *together* suggested the possible diagnosis of early onset sepsis, it sent an alert to the private physician, the nurse assigned to the patient, the pharmacist covering the patient's ward, and a fail safe alert to an assigned individual. In this case, it was to the infectious disease Fellow covering *at that moment in time.*"

At the mention of the ID Fellow, Dr. Michael Auginello leaned forward and scrutinized the program's capabilities. He was impressed. Alerts like this would be a great help to the infectious disease department. He'd been consulted too many times on cases where the infection had already overwhelmed the patient's immune system. An early intervention would have saved many of those patients. Maybe all of them.

"Not only will the program identify a potentially life threatening development in the patient's condition, it will also recommend *the preferred treatment options."*

Click.

An order set appeared outlining the requisite lab tests and treatment options, including sets of antibiotics. "Each set of antibiotics is tailored to the particular type of bacteria most likely to be infecting the patient."

Click.

"The program tracks antibiotic allergies and drug interactions. The instant that preliminary culture reports come in, the program alerts all relevant parties and recommends changes in antibiotic selection where indicated."

Now Dr. Auginello was doubly impressed. The alerts to change therapeutic options in real time was brilliant. A midnight result could lead to a call to the Infectious Disease Fellow and an immediate change in the treatment, not the next morning on rounds. He imagined what it would be like to never have to sit through another mortality review where the death had resulted from the delayed treatment of a systemic infection.

Reichart continued through a dozen more slides, outlining the program for admitting patients, allocating beds and scheduling procedures and tests, and the preferred length of stay. Then he hit them with the coup de grace.

"If there is one take home message from this presentation, it is this." He stepped to the front of the stage and raised a finger in the air. "Every physician in this facility has a moral, a legal and a fiduciary responsibility to optimize the income that accrues as a result of the care that you provide. And with the Croesus Patient Treatment Application, your use of computer-generated diagnostic terminology will significantly increase the income stream that you generate, because you will be choosing diagnoses that garner the *highest reimbursement allowed* by third party insurers."

He waited a moment for the words to sink in. Saw looks of skepticism and resentment on several faces. Reichart knew that for a hundred years physicians were never held accountable for the financial health of the hospital in which they practiced, only the health of the patients. Croesus's singular breakthrough in hospital management was to bind together physician practice, patient outcomes and financial rewards.

Asking for questions, a young physician from Family Medicine working without a tie asked about the rumors that Six North was being converted to an exclusive ward with special amenities.

"You are correct. We have revised the remodeling plans to convert the area into an executive suite for high income patients. We will offer them concierge service, meals ordered online 24/7, and for some, an expanded suite with a sitting room."

When the Family Medicine physician asked if that wasn't providing unequal levels of care, Reichart assured him that the *medical* care would be the same, only the amenities would be more plush. Sitting down, the young doctor muttered to his neighbor, "Croesus wants more Chestnut Hill, less Germantown."

Ending his presentation to a smattering of polite applause, Reichart said he had time for one or two questions. A few physicians expressed skepticism at the accuracy and safety of the computer-generated treatment plan. The president assured them that the Attending physician always had the last word on how the patient was to be treated.

When Reichart offered to answer one last question, Dr. Auginello stood up and introduced himself. Then he said that while he appreciated the effectiveness of alerting the ID team as soon as preliminary culture results were available, he was wary of employing a cookie-cutter approach to ordering the appropriate antibiotics. "If we have a resident strain of a pathogen with an unusual resistance pattern, we will want to recommend antibiotics that fit that particular pattern of susceptibility. Does your program allow for that?"

"It absolutely does. Our program allows for unique, hospital-specific variations," said Reichart. "The software analyzes the past three months of culture results and derives an ideal treatment plan.

It even distinguishes patterns of resistance in different wards. The ICU, for example, may harbor a unique strain that is not showing up in, say, L&D."

Sitting back down, Auginello found that he agreed, the system did have the potential to save a lot of lives. But he was still skeptical about giving up his independence, recalling the sage advice an old ID physician had imparted when Auginello first enrolled in the fellowship program. "The bugs don't read textbooks. Always expect the unexpected."

Dr. Auginello wasn't quite ready to believe that computers were quite as creative as human beings in thinking outside the box.

SIX

Mimi was standing at her portable computer logging in an intravenous drug she had just administered. She initialed the box in the ten am column and was about to confirm GIVEN when she heard a scream erupt a few doors down.

Startled, the nurse ran a few steps and looked in the doorway. She saw Mrs. Mudge on the floor beside her bed thrashing her head back and forth and screaming. Both side rails were elevated, as they were supposed to be. The nurse shook her head, appalled that the stubborn old woman had actually climbed *over* the rails. And for what?

"What are you doing in my bedroom? the patient cried. "Who are you? Why am I on the floor?"

Mimi called for Betty, the nurse's aide, to come help her. Together they lowered the bedside rails and grabbed the patient by the shoulders and the legs. But as they began to lift, the patient let out another blood curdling scream.

"Hold off," Mimi told the aide. "She might've broken her hip. We better wait for more help. You stay here and watch her."

The nurse ran to the station and paged the resident and the nursing supervisor STAT. Returning to the bedside, Mimi felt her throat constrict and her stomach tighten, anticipating the incident report she would have to make out, and knowing how the new bosses were quick to fire an employee for screwing up.

But it wasn't her fault. Mrs. Mudge hadn't been disoriented or confused, just *mean*. She was on her call button night and day! There was no good reason for her to climb *over* the side rail and fall to the floor.

So what the hell happened?

<><><><><><>

In the radiology department, the medical resident who had helped transport Mrs. Mudge studied the x-ray on the screen as the orthopedic Fellow pointed at the fracture in the femoral neck.

"Nasty break," muttered the bone surgeon. "It's gonna need an internal fixation."

"You'll put in a rod," said the medical resident.

"Yup. Gotta get out the old hammer and chisel. Insert a rod, some screws, a little bailing wire and she'll be good as new. It's no surprise, given her age and the arthritic changes in the hip, you can see them clearly on the x-ray"

"Which is pretty damn bad, considering her age and her co-morbidities."

"Afraid I can't help you with that soft organ stuff, I'm just an old hammer and chisel man. But I can get her on her feet again." He told the medical doctor to make the patient NPO after midnight, he was scheduling her for surgery in the morning. Then he called the physical therapy department and ordered a traction set up for the patient.

The medical resident looked through the glass window at the patient on the CAT scan table and cursed his luck to have to follow the patient through surgery, the orthopedic service having refused to take on primary responsibility for the patient. If the surgery went badly and the patient expired, the mortality review would still fall on medicine. It was a load of crap.

<><><><><><>

Once the patient was returned to her bed and her leg placed in traction, Mimi filled out the dreaded incident report. She detailed exactly what she had seen and done, including that the two side rails had both been up when the discovered the patient on the floor.

As the nursing supervisor looked over the report, Mimi

expressed her puzzlement that the woman seemed to be confused. "Mrs. Mudge didn't seem to know where she was or who I was," said Mimi. "She *always* knew who I am because she was always promising to get me written up."

"It seems the patient has finally gotten her wish," said the supervisor.

"I wonder if she hit her head. Could that bring on her confusion? I mean, it was so quick!"

"Be sure they conduct a thorough neurologic exam. She may need to go for a CAT scan of the head."

"That won't be easy, her leg is in traction."

"Then you'll just have to hold her leg and pull while they run the scan," said the supervisor. She told Mimi they would review the incident in the afternoon operations conference and give her their decision afterwards.

"*Decision*? What kind of decision?" asked Mimi.

"Whether or not you are liable for the injury to your patient."

The supervisor left, leaving Mimi depressed and scared. She needed this job, her husband had been laid off from his warehouse job and had only been able to find occasional temp work. With no benefits. If she couldn't find another job as a nurse, they would be in deep shit.

If only she knew someone who could help her keep her job. Lawyers were so expensive.

SEVEN

On advice from Mrs. Mudge's nurse and after conferring with his Fellow, the medical resident paged the neurology services for a consultation about Mrs. Mudge's confusion. After a long wait and a second page, the Neuro resident called back. "Is this a STAT consult?" he asked. "Is she seizing? I'm up to my armpits in consults."

The medical resident told him the patient was not seizing, just confused.

"Okay, get a CAT scan of the head and we'll put her on the list."

"But I can't take her down to radiology, she's in traction."

"That's your problem. There's no point our seeing the patient without the scan. Get it done, then page the intern on call for our service, he'll review the films."

The medical resident was about to explain that his patient was a pre-op who needed evaluation before surgery in the morning, but the neurology resident had already hung up on him.

Giving up, he entered a note in the chart: *Neuro requesting CT of head; will see patient after scan in completed.* The medical resident wished he'd told Neuro about the surgery being scheduled for the morning. But there were so many details to sweat, and this was his first month in the rotation. He couldn't keep *everything* straight in his head.

Well, he would just have to prioritize. Next thing was, carry the scan request to radiology, explain the patient was scheduled for emergency surgery and beg them to scan her head *today.*

He wasn't looking forward to standing in the CAT scan being exposed to all that radiation while pulling on the traction. And this was only his first year in residency! Would his testicles end up completely fried by the end of his third year?

<><><><><><>

As his shift came to an end, Lenny hung up his mop and rinsed his bucket, relieved that no more complaints had come his way. He'd made a good start on the collection for Louie's widow. As to the new camera over the time clock and the rules about clocking in, there wasn't much he could do about that. He had to pick his fights, and that was one he couldn't win.

Descending the stairs to the basement, he stepped into the housekeeping locker room, where he found Abrahm polishing his black work shoes. The rag snapped with the rhythm of a shoeshine vendor, leaving a glossy shine.

"Hey, Abraham Lincoln!" Lenny called to him. "Are those another pair of Russian shoes?"

"How are yu, George Wushington?" Abrahm replied. "Yes, these are shoes from Tula. Vury fine leather. The best."

Putting his work shoes in the locker, Abrahm fished out an envelope stuffed with dollar bills and handed it to Lenny. "For Louie. May he rest in peace."

"Thank you, Abrahm, you're a good man."

"The collection, it is going goodt?"

"Yeah, people are generous. Word got out so fast about him, I didn't hardly have to explain a thing."

"Turruble thing, to take your life. Turrible."

At the despised time clock Abrahm took his card from the rack and waved it in front of the new camera as though performing a magic trick on stage. In a theatrical gesture he slowly brought his card to the mouth of the clock and jabbed it into the device, where it triggered a *click*. Then he pulled the card out and with a flourish inserted it back in the rack.

"Too bad we can not put glue in the clock again," said Abrahm, referring to the day when an angry worker in the laundry squeezed glue into the time clock, destroying it, a victory still celebrated years later.

"No, I'm afraid those days are gone, the camera is here to say," said Lenny.

At the hospital's main entrance Lenny saw his wife Patience chatting with a co-worker, and he marveled, as he so often did, at her slim figure, her lovely face and smooth, cocoa skin. He told himself for the thousandth time he was one lucky son of a bitch. An ugly white guy who pushed a mop for a living married to this African princess of a lady.

They walked together down the broad steps and to the employee parking lot. Lenny opened the door for her, one of his rare concessions to gallantry, and enjoyed the *thunk* of the old car door as it closed. The vehicle had been his dad's, and he hated to part with it. But with the car going on fifteen years old, he knew it was time to give it up.

"How was your day?" Patience asked as he maneuvered the car along Germantown Ave, the wheels rattling over the cobblestones and the old steel tracks, the trolley now long taken out of service.

"The usual hell. I've got six new grievances just today."

"Six? I hope you're not trying to handle them all by yourself."

"No, Regis has three and Moose took two. I'll be their backup." He waited patiently while a bus pulled out from its stop and lumbered up the avenue. "They put up a camera over our time clock. It's gonna take pictures as we punch in and out so nobody can sign somebody else in."

"Can they do that?"

"Yeah. There's nothing in the contract or the law to stop them."

"That's such a shame. These new owners are greedy bastards, aren't they?"

Lenny shrugged. Her comment required no answer; they both knew what they were up against.

As he drove toward their home in Mt. Airy, Lenny thought about Louie, lying in a cold locker at the Medical Examiner's. Lenny had been in the hospital cadaver fridge more than once, happily never quite becoming a corpse, although he'd come awfully close more times than he cared to remember. He recalled the day he'd been shot in the hospital parking lot, and how a few days later the killer had ripped open his fresh surgical wound. The old weariness threatened to open up and swallow him, but he fought it back down. There was too much at stake now to withdraw into a funk.

"Pizza for dinner?" he asked, not wanting to cook.

"The kids will like that. I'll call in the order."

"Don't forget the garlic bread."

"Of course," Patience said. "And double sausage for you and Malcolm. Takia and I will have the Caesar salad with chicken."

Lenny grumbled, not wanting to be reminded of his wife and daughter's healthy eating habits. Somebody had to hold down the right to eat good old fashioned American red meat, and he was bound to do it.

EIGHT

The anesthesia intern, fresh out of school and not wanting to screw up any of his first cases, reviewed Mrs. Mudge's chart in preparation for the surgery the following morning. He had seven cases to review, and he was hungry, having missed lunch in order to cover on a long case at noon.

The intern found a list of the patient's home medications, as well as a list of her current meds. There was nothing in either list that would interfere with the surgery. The anesthesia should be uneventful.

Going to her room for the pre-op interview, he found the patient sitting in bed with eyes closed, apparently asleep, one leg in traction. Calling her name, Mrs. Mudge slowly opened her eyes and turned to look at him, saying not a word.

"Hi," said the anesthesia intern. "I'm here to ask you some questions so you can go to surgery in the morning. Okay? Is that all right?"

The patient nodded her head.

The intern read off the list of her home medications, asking if they were correct. She nodded her head yes. He asked if there were any other medications that she was in the habit of taking.

The patient shook her head no.

"You don't take aspirin or Motrin or any other over the counter pain medications?"

"Why would I take them? I'm not a cripple!" said Mudge.

"Of course. I just need to be sure you're not on something we don't know about." He looked at the history in the chart one more time. "What about alcohol? Are you in the habit of enjoying a cocktail in the evening? A glass of wine, perhaps?"

"I don't drink!"

"Oh, okay. No alcohol, no over the counter N-saids. Good.

What about allergies? Did you ever react to a medication? Break out in a rash, anything like that?"

She shook her head.

Looking at his watch, the intern thought about the six other patients he had to interview and decided he'd covered all the bases. Besides, the ortho surgeons would obtain their own pre-op review. If there was anything he'd missed, they would certainly uncover it.

He signed off on the pre-op review, closed the chart and hurried to find his next patient.

<><><><><><>

Dr. Slocum slumped in his thick leather chair and massaged his temples. Miss Burgess, sitting opposite him, shook her head.

"Headache still bad?" she asked.

"Worse. Reichart told me that I have to convince the Attendings to go along with the new computerized diagnostic and treatment program or I'll be out of a job."

"Well then your future is assured. The program is a godsend. It makes the doctor's job so easy, any idiot could do it."

"That's the problem. We can't suggest that the program is smarter than the physicians. They *hate* when a protocol-driven program usurps their autonomy."

"Just keep reminding them it will mean fewer law suits and more revenues. They'll come around."

"I hope to god they do." He abandoned trying to reduce the headache. "What about you? Anything bad happening among your girls?"

"A patient fell out of bed and fractured her hip."

"Ouch. Was she confused? Did the nurses have her on a one-to-one safety watch?"

"She supposedly hadn't shown signs of confusion until she went over the side. But I suspect somebody failed to do a proper neurologic assessment."

"Hmm. What are you doing about the nurse assigned to her?"

"I was going to terminate her as an example, but decided to just put her on probation. What do you think?"

"Well, Croesus wants us to get rid of the senior nurses, they cost a lot more than the new grads and they have a stubborn streak of independence."

"She's only been with us two years. And she graduated from our own nursing program."

"You did the right thing. Firing a nurse without a clear case of negligence would ruffle too many feathers."

"Good. I'll give her six months probation. That will put the fear of god into her and the others."

"Excellent." Slocum patted Burgess's hand, noting the lack of a wedding ring and the slender gold band on his own hand. "We make a good team, you and me."

"We do."

"Let's hope Croesus keeps us both on. Be a shame to break up a matching set."

Burgess looked into Slocum's eyes, smiled sweetly and wished she knew a foolproof way to get rid of his wife without leaving a trace of evidence behind.

<><><><><>

Mimi was struggling to enter all her patient data in the new computerized charting system. She input the patient's blood pressure, pulse, respirations and temperature, then she searched for the *enter* button, but couldn't find it. Finally she realized the numbers were automatically recorded. But then she realized she'd typed in the wrong temperature, having read the numbers of another patient from the paper the nurse's aide had given her.

How do you correct the number, she wondered. There must be *some* way to fix it. She was trying different drop down menus, none of which allowed her to make a change, when she heard someone cough behind her. Turning around, Mimi's heart sank, seeing the nursing supervisor standing there with a paper in her hand.

This is it. I'm out of a job.

The supervisor handed Mimi the paper, saying, "I need your signature on the bottom."

Mimi tightened all her muscles as she forced her eyes to read the document. A wave of relief came over her when she got to the section labeled DISCIPLINARY ACTION -

SIX MONTH PROBATION. ANY SUBSEQUENT TRANSGRESSION WILL RESULT IN IMMEDIATE SUSPENSION AND POTENTIAL TERMINATION.

Well, at least she wasn't out of a job. Yet. She would have to be careful and not screw up any more. It wasn't fair, but there it was.

"Sign at the bottom, please, I have to finish my rounds."

"Uh, do I get a copy of this?"

"I will make a copy and leave it with you before I go off duty."

Feeling like the victim of a rape, Mimi signed her name, then printed it again in neat block letters. The supervisor pulled it from her fingers and hurried off the ward, leaving Mimi feeling wounded and alone.

<><><><><><>

At eight pm a harried neurology intern knocked on the door to Mrs. Mudge's room and entered, anxious to complete the last consult of the day. He found an attractive, middle aged woman seated at the bedside reading a fashion magazine.

"Excuse me," said the intern.

The visitor looked up and smiled a radiant smile. "Yes, doctor. May I help you?"

"Uh, yes. Are you related to Mrs., um..." He referred to the name on the consult sheet. "Mrs. Harriet Mudge?"

"I am her daughter."

"Oh, excellent. I just came from reviewing her CAT scan with my Attending and the radiologist. There was no evidence of a stroke, no need for you to be concerned."

"Why would my mother be tested for a stroke when she broke her hip falling out of bed?" The daughter's smile was replaced by an angry frown. "Did she hit her head when she fell? Nobody told me about her hitting her head."

"No, no, it was nothing like that. There were no external signs of head trauma. The nurse found your mom was confused this morning. We wanted to rule out a stroke as the cause of the confusion."

"I see. Well, if there was no sign of a stroke and she didn't hit her head, why was she confused?"

Unable to answer the question, the intern suggested that a thorough history might shed some light on the matter. He asked the daughter if her mother was in the habit of taking any prescription pain pills or tranquilizers. The daughter said no.

"What about over the counter pain pills? Aspirin. Mortrin. That sort of thing."

"Well I do know mother swore by aspirin. She called it the wonderest wonder drug. Mother took it regularly for her arthritis."

"Arthritis?"

"Yes. In the hip."

The intern made a note in the consult sheet. "What about alcohol? Did she enjoy a drink on a regular basis?"

"*Oh*, yes. I call mother every evening at five-thirty when I leave work, and she always has her cocktail before her dinner."

"Just one."

"I don't doubt she often has a second, judging by the gallon bottles of bourbon she buys. Sometimes mom's in quite good spirits when I call."

The intern completed the consult note, carefully recording and underlying the likely abuse of alcohol and aspirin. He signed it and hurried off to find the Fellow, who would have to check the note and co-sign it before it was put in the chart.

Finding his Fellow about to perform a lumbar puncture, the intern asked if he could read the consult note to him. The Fellow told him to leave the consult in his lab coat pocket, he would look it over when he was done.

"Should I wait around until you're finished here?"

"No need, you can go home. " As the intern turned to go, the Fellow called after him, "Be at rounds at six am sharp!"

Hurrying to the parking lot, he texted his girlfriend that he was on the way to the pub. Driving down Germantown Ave, the neurology intern wondered how the surgeon would compensate for the anti-coagulating effects of alcohol *and* aspirin. He remembered that alcohol abuse impaired the liver's production of clotting factors. Aspirin, if he remembered correctly, reduced the ability of the platelet to clump and begin forming a clot.

Well, they weren't his problems. He had noted both problems clearly in his consultation note. It was up to the surgeons to perform the operation in a safe manner. That's why they made the big bucks.

NINE

The orthopedic surgeon stood still while his assistant snapped on the helmet to his operating outfit. It contained a sealed breathing unit, so that none of the micro-organisms released when he spoke, coughed or sneezed could possibly be dispersed in the air and enter the deep wound he was about to open in Mrs. Mudge's hip. The circulating air in the room was scrubbed twelve times an hour, further reducing the amount of bacteria and fungi carried on the air currents.

While the circulating nurse finished setting the instruments out on a long table, like an elaborate dinner set for an aristocrat's dinner party, the surgeon listened as an assistant read off a long check list. After each category, someone on the team called out "check."

Satisfied that all the preparations for the first case of the day were in place, the surgeon allowed his senior resident to make the opening incision. The scalpel shone in the harsh fluorescent lights like a miniature sword in battle. The chief surgeon smiled. He liked to think of himself as a warrior doing battle against disease. His hammers and saws, metal rods and artificial joints were like the weapons and armor of old.

As the resident pried open the incision, several small vessels began oozing blood. The young physician applied a hot electric probe to the edges of the wound. The bleeding slowed, but did not stop.

"Apply more cautery" the Attending instructed. With his sealed breathing apparatus he could not smell the burning flesh from the cautery.

The resident did as he was told. The bleeding slowed further but did not stop entirely.

"Any problems with her coags?" the senior surgeon asked. The circulating nurse had already read off the patient's coagulation studies and platelet count, two measures of the ability of the patient's blood to clot. Both had been normal. But the senior surgeon wanted to go over everything again, just to be sure.

"Read me her History and Physical and her medications. And the anesthesia assessment."

The nurse read all the entries. There was nothing in the patient record or her lab values to suggest the patient had a problem with bleeding.

Satisfied, he instructed the resident to continue with the incision. With the femur exposed, the surgeon inspected the fracture line and called for the rod and the hammer. He had the rod driven half way into the bone when the anesthesia resident told him he was getting coffee ground material out of the naso-gastric tube.

"Jesus Christ! Don't tell me she has a GI bleed! What the hell's going on here?"

The anesthesia resident said there was no frank blood in the tube, so it didn't look like an active bleed. Realizing he had gone past the point of no return, the surgeon ordered fresh frozen plasma in case the bleeding became severe. then he raised his arm and struck another blow with the hammer.

<><><><><><>

Lenny was mopping the floor of a patient's room when he saw the tall, lanky figure of Dr. Michael Auginello standing in the doorway.

"Hey, doc. How's it goin'?" Lenny had a special fondness for the Infectious Disease doctor, having worked with him on a number of murder investigations over the years.

"Hello, Lenny. How are things in your neck of the woods?" The physician stopped in mid-sentence and sniffed the air in the room. "Hey. Why don't I smell any bleach? You're supposed to clean the rooms of the C. diff patients with bleach. I went over this with your departmental director last month."

"Yeah, I read the memo. And that's the first thing I asked for this morning when I was collecting my equipment, but they wouldn't give it to me. Said it had to be approved by the director, and he wasn't in yet."

"For god's sake, why do you need his approval?"

"The bleach products are more expensive than the regular detergents and they can damage the floors."

Auginello sighed. He had been fighting the bean counters ever since he came to James Madison. The administration couldn't get it through their bureaucratic heads that every extra dollar spent on environmental services saved them *four* dollars in hospital acquired infection costs.

"I'll send him another email and c-c the chief medical officer. I frankly don't now what else to do."

As the physcian turned to go, Mimi stopped him, having heard his conversation with Lenny, "Can I ask you something, Doctor Auginello?" she said.

"Sure. What's up, Mimi?"

"I was just thinking. Us nurses and the housekeepers clean the room and the equipment of the C. diff patients with a bleach product. Right?"

"Yes, that's right."

"Well if we clean the patient's *room* with bleach, 'cause it's the only thing that'll kill the spores, how come we don't clean the patient the same way? I mean, their skin is bound to have the same spores on them that we're killing on hard surfaces. Right?"

Auginello stuck his tongue in his cheek and considered the proposition. "It's true, researchers have captured C. diff spores from swabs of the patient's skin. No doubt they are continually auto-inoculating and re-seeding their GI tract." He wondered aloud what the effect would be on the patient's skin, since the bleach they used sometimes took out the color of the surface it was used on.

"We swim in the hospital pool," said Lenny. "That's loaded with bleach."

"And we've used a Dakins solution to irrigate wounds for decades," Mimi added. "That's got bleach in it, you can smell it when you pour it on the dressing."

Auginello remembered for the hundredth time why he had so much respect for the nurses and housekeepers on Seven South. Especially Mimi and Lenny. "I'll have to do a literature search and see if anybody's done any studies of the practice. I'll let you know." The physician ambled off humming an old jazz standard, happy to have a question to study and ponder. There was nothing like the prospect of a good, old fashioned research project to brighten his day.

TEN

The orthopedic surgeon was growing increasingly worried about the excessive bleeding from Mrs. Mudge's wound. He had hammered the rod into the bone and was beginning to close the wound, but the tissues kept oozing blood.

"Are you sure we're not missing something?" he called to the rest of the team. The anesthesia resident confirmed he knew of no reason for the bleeding. The circulating nurse went through the history and physical again and found nothing.

"What about the consults?"

"There are no consults in the chart, doctor," said the nurse. "Other than yours."

"I was told Neuro was consulted for her confusion. She had a CAT scan of the head, didn't she?"

The nurse checked the orders. "Yes, there's a consult ordered, but it's not in the chart."

"Neurology. Typical banker's hours. They're probably up in the room right now scratching their ass wondering where the patient is." He ordered another unit of fresh plasma, a unit of cryoprecipitate and ten units of platelet. When the blood bank department balked at releasing the platelets, given the patient went into the operating room with a normal platelet level, the surgeon yelled, "Put the bastard on speaker phone!"

Hearing the blood bank technician's voice, the surgeon yelled, "Now get this straight! I've got my hands inside a wound that is bleeding profusely and shows no signs of stopping. *I have no idea why*. But rather than stand here and watch my patient continue to hemorrhage, I'm willing to try *anything*. *Anything* that might stop the bleeding, because I can't close this wound as long as I have a bleeding problem, and the patient cannot remain on the table under general anesthesia until the cows come home and you people get your heads out of your ass!"

The blood bank technician agreed to release the platelets and send them up STAT. Satisfied, the surgeon turned back to his patient, vowing to find out who was responsible for this mess and have his head.

<><><><><>

The NASH survey team returned to the seventh floor with Miss Burgess and the housekeeping supervisor in tow. Today they were conducting a "continuum of care" review, looking at how information and orders are carried through as the patient moves from the ER to the ward and to the various treatment and diagnostic areas.

They passed Lenny, who was mopping the floor, a yellow caution sign placed at the end of a section of wet floor. Reaching the patient on isolation they had visited the day before, Miss Wiggins stuck her head into the room and sniffed the air. "I am glad to note you have supplied the bleach for this patient," she said to the housekeeping supervisor.

"Always," he replied. "As soon as we get the request from infection control, we send the product right up."

In the next room Miss Wiggins spotted an empty bed and asked where the patient had gone. Mimi explained that Mrs. Mudge had gone to surgery and would probably be transferred to the orthopedic ward.

"Ah, you took an ortho patient as an overflow," said Wiggins.

"Not exactly," said Burgess, squirming at having to confess to the surveyor that a patient had been injured from a fall. Raising a single eyebrow in disapproval, Wiggins informed Burgess they would review the patient chart in the Recovery Room after lunch, and moved on.

Burgess slipped away for a moment and alerted the nursing supervisor for surgical services that the NASH surveyors would be looking at Mrs. Mudge's chart and told her to be sure everything was up to date. Then she caught up with the surveyors.

ELEVEN

Mimi struggled to sign off all her ten o'clock medications in the new computer program. One patient had refused his meds. The nurse notified the physician and asked him to intervene, but now she wasn't sure how to make the entry in the new program. If the meds were not given on time, a red flag appeared and the pharmacy supervisor was alerted. Mimi didn't want to see a red flag a day after she was put on probation. But she couldn't figure out how to stop the damn icon from appearing.

After trying several drop down menu choices, she found an entry labeled MEDICATION HELD. A window opened where she could write an explanation of the event and who she notified about it. Happy at finding the choice, she typed in her explanation and selected SAVE. As the screen returned to the medication schedule, a red flag popped up in the ten am box.

Afraid her probation would be in jeopardy, she gave in to her last desperate option: she paged her supervisor. As she waited for the woman to call, Mimi was told to strip Mrs. Mudge's bed and have it cleaned for a new admission, the woman was not coming back to Seven South.

The nurse hoped the woman had gotten through the surgery all right. She shuddered to think what would happen to her if Mrs. Mudge died as a result of her fall. Forget about being terminated from James Madison; she would be lucky to hold onto her license to practice nursing.

<><><><><><>

While listening to the report from the anesthesiologist, the Recovery Room nurse took a quick look at the bulky dressing over Mrs. Mudge's hip. It was 'clean and dry,' as the nurses liked to write in their notes. Informed of the bleeding problems that happened in the OR, she made a mental note to check the white dressing every fifteen minutes for signs of bleeding.

As the recovery room nurse began her patient assessment, her supervisor came in and scooped up the chart. "Any problems in the OR?" she asked the staff nurse.

"She had some intra-op bleeding. They had to give her frozen plasma and platelets. But she's okay now. I'm going to repeat the H&H in an hour."

"The NASH team heard about this one's slip and fall. They'll be down some time to review the case. We have to make sure the chart is complete and all our T's are crossed."

The nursing supervisor put on the reading glasses dangling on a bejeweled string around her neck and began to thumb though the chart. Checking to see that all of the doctor's orders had been duly carried out, she was relieved that all of the medication orders had been administered on time. Good. But when she followed all the consultation orders, the supervisor was surprised to see that there was no neurology consult in the chart.

"Where is the note from neurology?" she asked the OR nurse. "Do you have it?"

"Me? No. Why would I have a consult? It should be in the chart."

Growing alarmed that the NASH team would discover an incomplete record, the supervisor paged the neurology team with a '911' added to the call-back number.

A minute later an annoyed Neurology resident called, demanding to know what was the emergency. The nursing supervisor explained she had to have Mrs. Mudge's consultation in the chart at once, the NASH survey team was on their was down to the Recovery Room.

When the resident balked, complaining he couldn't leave clinic for at least two hours, the supervisor warned him she would call the Chair of his department and report the resident for placing the hospital's accreditation at risk if somebody didn't immediately bring the consultation note to Recovery. Cursing under his breath, the resident promised to come right down with the document.

Five minutes later an angry neurology resident hurried into the Recovery Room. He whipped out a copy of the consultation note and dropped it into the chart without bothering to place it in the appropriate section. The nursing supervisor moved it to its proper place behind the consultation tab and read the report. Although the handwriting was hard to read and the Attending physician's signature illegible, with no name printed or stamped beneath it, the essential elements of the consult were plain to see.

Plain, and to a nursing supervisor, terrifying.

The neurology resident had clearly noted that the patient likely had abused aspirin and alcohol for some time. This made her doubly at risk of bleeding during surgery, or after. Yet neither the anesthesia nor the surgical pre-op assessment made any mention of these two major risks.

Making matters worse, the consultation note was not dated and timed, an omission all too common among consulting physicians. There was no documentation that the consult had been carried out *before* the surgery. Knowing that the NASH team would suspect that the consultation had been conducted *after* the operation, the supervisor took out her pen and entered yesterday's date and a time of two-twenty pm, which was within the two hour guideline that the hospital administration had stipulated for all consultations.

The nursing supervisor instructed the nurse to page the orthopedic Attending and alert him to the patient's history of alcohol and aspirin use. "I hope to god he knows about it already," she said. "But if he doesn't, at least he'll be ready when the NASH people interview him."

The Recovery nurse shook her head as she paged the surgeon. It was an old story, all too familiar to her. Physicians just did not consistently communicate across disciplines. But then, neither did nurses.

TWELVE

The Orthopedic Attending surgeon barreled into the Recovery Room and marched up to the bed where the anesthesia resident was standing beside his post-op patient. "What's this I hear about my patient abusing aspiring? *And* alcohol? *Why wasn't I made aware of this before starting the case?*"

The anesthesia resident protested that he had interviewed the patient, and she had said nothing about abusing aspirin, or alcohol.

"And you *believed* her? A confused, non-compos mentis patient? Are you an idiot or just lazy?"

Declining to answer the rhetorical question, the anesthesia resident pointed to the neurology consultation and complained that it hadn't been in the chart when he interviewed the patient. "If Neuro can't get their consults in the chart in a timely fashion, I can't be held responsible."

The Attending surgeon turned a blistering gaze at the orthopedic resident who had conducted the pre-op assessment. The junior surgeon confirmed that the Neurology consult had not been in the chart the night before, *or* this morning. "Remember we reviewed the chart in the OR *twice*. Once right before starting the case at the time out, and once again intra-op when we ran into a little bleeding."

The Attending did not comment on the euphemism "a little bleeding." Instead, he pointed out that if a lowly Neurology intern could uncover such critically relevant information, there was no excuse for anesthesia *and* surgery failing to discover the same relevant facts.

With no choice but to deal with the complications that could develop in his patient, he ordered his resident to page the ICU team. He wanted his patient in the ICU under the direct care of a critical care physician. And he wanted her transferred to the critical care unit. *NOW*.

<><><><><><>

In the sewing room, Lenny dipped his soft pretzel in a cup of coffee and took a ferocious bite. "I've never seen it this bad," he said, his mouth half full of pretzel. "Six disciplines given out in one day. It's fricking ridiculous."

"We got t' get them to cut this shit out," said Moose. "These Croesus people just want to cut and cut. Any excuse to fire somebody, they take it."

Birdie snipped a thread and put down her heavy duty shears. "Where's the union in all this, Lenny? Can't they come down here and tell us what they're gonna do about it?"

Lenny agreed, the area rep should come down and give a presentation to the rank and file about how they were going to fight the recent slew of attacks. It was one thing to apply the rules; it was altogether different to fire people right and left. They were attacking workers who had been at James Madison for years. Decades, even.

"I called and asked the union to arrange a membership meeting," said Lenny. "We definitely need to come up with a plan. You know what the hospital administrator said? The VP for Operations said he wasn't going to give us the auditorium to hold a meeting."

"That's a violation of the contract! Ain't it?" said Little Mary.

"Yes and no. We're entitled to a certain number of meetings a year, but the contract doesn't specify *when* they have to occur. The administration is claiming the auditorium is fully booked until next month."

"It's outrageous," said Birdie. "Where do they get the nerve to say stuff like that?"

"Those Croesus bosses have no shame," said Lenny. "None whatsoever."

He took a last mouthful of pretzel and was chewing it slowly, ruminating on the mess they were all in, when the door opened and Abrahm came in. He was holding a piece of paper with printing on it. When a worker brought him a document it was usually trouble.

"Len'nye, please to look at this. I think it is vury bad news."

Lenny took the paper and scanned it quickly.

"Those bastards," he said. "I never thought they'd sink this low. *Bastards*!"

Everyone crowded around Lenny to look over his shoulder to see what had made him so upset. It was a document the likes of which none of them had ever seen before. Not even Lenny.

THIRTEEN

Holding the document that Abrahm had brought into the sewing room, Lenny looked at his friends and said, "Croesus has initiated a campaign to decertify the union."

They stared back, unsure what Lenny was talking about. Birdie asked him to explain what it was about.

"It's a petition to dump our union. It's supposedly put out by the 'Committee to Save James Madison.' If they get thirty per cent of the union members to sign the petition, the NLRB holds an election. If they get fifty per cent of the votes, the union is history."

Moose slammed a big fist into an open palm, his black eyes wide with fury. "Croesus can't get away with it, can they? It ain't legal. It can't be!"

"By law the administration is barred from sponsoring a decertification petition. But I'm sure they're the ones really behind it."

"But if the union is stopped from representing us, who will?"

"That's the point. Nobody." He went on to explain that usually union members launched a decertification campaign when they thought their union was corrupt and they wanted to replace it with a better one. "But in this case, the goal is to leave us with no union at all."

"Nobody looking out for us," said Moose. "No one to stand up to the boss."

"That's it," said Lenny. "We would be a right to work company, without a union."

"Right to work, work with no rights is more like it," said Moose. "I don't see how can they get away with it!"

"They're hiding behind the bogus committee that's named at the bottom. The petition says Croesus can only keep the hospital open if we give up all the 'restrictions and inefficiencies' that the union imposes. They're saying the hospital has to become *streamlined* and *efficient* if it's going to compete in the *new marketplace of health care services.*"

"Yeah, right," said Birdie. "They want us to give up things like safety procedures that keep us from gettin' AIDS. Back in the day I used t' get stuck all the time from needles folks left in the linen. I ain't been stuck in a long time on account of the new safety needles they brought in."

"Health and safety go out the window when the union is broken," said Lenny. "That's got to be our argument. Not just for the workers, but the patients, too."

Lenny knew that keeping the union would be the toughest fight of his life. Harder than crossing swords with a killer. Harder than surviving a stay in the intensive care unit. It was a fight for survival for the entire membership, and the patients.

He suggested that they try to get a sense of how many would sign the petition. They would survey their co-workers; try to determine which departments were most vulnerable. Then they would put out a petition of their own explaining why decertifying the union would be a bad deal for everybody.

"The union's got t' call a meeting now! They got to!," said Little Mary. "'Cause I got a whole lotta things on my mind I want to talk about."

"Of course we'll have a general meeting. I'll call the area representative as soon as I get back to my work area and fill him in. If the hospital doesn't give us the big auditorium, we can meet in Center City at the union hall."

The meeting broke up with everyone angry and fired up to stop the campaign, Lenny most of all. Having engaged in many investigations over the years, he realized this one would be the most critical one of all: he had to find proof that Croesus was behind the decert program. It was the only way to be sure they would win the vote.

He just had no idea which rock was concealing that particular poisonous snake.

<><><><><><>

Miss Wiggins and her survey partner entered the Recovery Room and asked to see Mrs. Mudge's chart. The nursing supervisor for the OR gave her the chart and settled her at the nurse's station. Wiggins traced the patient's progress from her initial visit to the Emergency Room, her assessment by the triage nurse and the ER physician, and her referral to a medical doctor.

"I see the triage nurse recorded the home medications, and the medical service seems to have copied it word for word."

The supervisor suggested that it was only logical that the second assessment came up with the same drugs.

"And listed them in the same order?" said Wiggins, a skeptical look on her face. She reviewed the nursing notes describing the fall and the hip fracture. "I want to see a copy of the incident report," she said. The supervisor promised to get her a copy.

Wiggins carefully went over the assessments made by medicine, surgery and neurology, stopping to scrutinize the neurology note's mention of the patient's aspirin and alcohol use. She noted that the pre-operative notes from surgery and anesthesia did not comment on neurology's obervation.

Turning to the anesthesia resident, who was evaluating another patient, Miss Wiggins asked why the omission. The anesthesia resident told her they had discussed the issues prior to starting the case. "You can see Dr. Taylor ordered fresh frozen plasma before starting the case. We were fully prepared for any excessive bleeding that might occur."

"And did it?"

The anesthesia resident reluctantly admitted there had been a bit of bleeding during the procedure, but it had been controlled and posed no risk to the patient.

Casting a skeptical eye on the young doctor, Miss Wiggins closed the chart and handed it back to the OR supervisor, who uttered a silent prayer that they wouldn't be cited for failing to recognize a critical risk to a patient facing surgery. A NASH citation would put everyone involved in the case, including the nurses, in danger of losing their jobs.

<><><><><><>

Not long after the NASH survey team left, the Recovery Room Nurse called the orthopedic resident over to see Mrs. Mudge. Asked what seems to be the trouble, the nurse pointed out the patient's heart rate, which was a bit high. Then she showed him a tiny smear on a cardboard test strip. The smear was black around the edges and vividly blue in the middle.

"When I saw the H&H was low but I didn't see a whole lot of bleeding from the wound, I figured I ought to test her stool for blood, and it came back positive. See?"

The young surgeon felt a lump in his throat as he looked once more at the black stool on the test with the vivid blue color. If the patient had a clotting problem that was causing her to bleed into her GI tract, she could easily be losing blood somewhere else as well. Like into her newly repaired hip.

"I'll notify Dr. Taylor about the GI bleed. Give her two units of blood and a unit of fresh frozen plasma." Stepping to the station to call his chief, the resident added, "Oh, and you better page the critical care service. We'll be moving this patient to the ICU in, like, five minutes."

FOURTEEN

Nurse Gary Tuttle was in the ICU caring for Mr. Burns, an eighty-five years old gentleman with a history of colon cancer that had recurred and spread to his liver and kidneys. The patient required mechanical ventilation with a high oxygen content, a bad prognostic sign. During rounds Gary had heard the ICU Chief say that the patient's prognosis was less than zero.

As he was mixing an intravenous anti-ulcer drug and filling out the label, he noted a young darkly complected man with a little pointed goatee standing at the bedside talking to Mr. Burns. Gary went to ask if the young man had any questions.

"No thanks, man, I'm cool," said the young man, leaning on the bedside rail. "It's okay I talk to my gran-dad, isn't it? I mean, he can hear me, can't he?"

"I'm giving him a light sedation, so he's not going to answer your questions or look at you. But often patients tell us when we stop the sedation and pull out the breathing tube that they heard many of the conversations going on around the bed."

"Okay, cool. Thanks."

Gary went back to preparing the IV medication. He was a sandy haired man, a tad over weight, with pale blue eyes and a gentle demeanor. Finishing with the mixing, he carried the drug to the bedside and hung it on the pole, ready to be administered at the appropriate time.

"My gran, he's a war hero. You know that?" said the young man.

"Is that right?" said the nurse.

"Sure is. He was in the navy in the second world war. Yup. He was only *fifteen* years old, but he was big for his age and he lied about when he was born." The grandson took the patient's hand in his.

"There weren't too many blacks in the navy back then. Mostly they loaded munitions, on account it was the most dangerous duty on the ship."

The grandson gently rotated the old man's arm, revealing the inner aspect. "See that anchor tattoo? It means he was a navy man. Served in the Pacific. He rescued a whole bunch a' marines they were transporting when their ship went down. Got two medals for it. One for bravery, one for being injured."

Gary looked at the face of the patient, his eyes closed due to the sedation, and realized he had not said a single word to the man all morning. He felt a little ashamed, having treated his patient like an inanimate object: a heart, a lung, kidneys and liver.

"I wonder," said Gary aloud. The young man looked at him. "I was just thinking Do you have any pictures of Mister Burns from when he was in the service?"

"Sure, I got lots a them. I scanned a bunch a' pics and loaded them in my cell phone. Take a look." He pulled out his phone and ran through the photographs.

"Would you be willing to print a few of them out and make a little picture album? Nothing fancy. Just a few pictures and an explanation of what he was doing and where they were taken."

"Sure I can. You want me to bring it here to the hospital?"

"Yes, I do. I was thinking, maybe it's won't really make a difference in how we care for your grandfather, but if I saw the pictures from his youth and learned something about who he was, I think I might treat him a little more, I don't know, more kindly. Not that I'm not kind to him."

"Sure, sure, I get it. He'd be more a person. I mean, I bet you never even talked to him. Not once."

"That's exactly the problem. Mister Burns was intubated in the Emergency Room and came up here sedated, so I never heard his voice. I never got to know him."

The young man promised to return the next day with the album and ambled out of the ICU.

Pleased with his idea, Gary straightened the top sheet over Mr.

Burns, then he joined Dr. Fahim, the Chief of the ICU, at the bedside of his other patient, Mrs. Mudge. Fahim was listening while his critical care Fellow read off the latest lab results. Mudge had received one unit of blood in the Recovery Room and was receiving the second unit as they spoke. Fahim stood with his arms crossed over his chest, his dark eyes staring at the patient, who was sedated and breathing with support from a ventilator.

"It is un-believable," he said, pointing at the patient. "How could they take the patient to surgery without first correcting her aspirin induced bleeding disorder?" No one on his team replied, knowing it was a rhetorical question. "And not to treat her impending alcohol withdrawal — that is criminal. *Criminal!*"

He turned to nurse Gary Tuttle and asked about the patient's urine output.

"Ten cc's in the last hour," said Gary. Reading the computer program's data analysis, the Fellow reported that the new program suggested they send a spot urine for sodium and electrolytes. He leaned closer and read more text. "If the sodium is elevated, collect urine for twenty-four hours and administer Lasix forty milligrams."

Fahim shook his head, his black eyes smoldering. "The new regime thinks I'm not smart enough to recognize acute renal failure! They think they can replace me with a *robot* physician? Ridiculous!"

He stood another moment in front of the bed pondering the situation. "I want a bleeding time study." Turning to the residents, medical students and pharmacy intern rounding with him, Fahim asked if any of them had ever conducted a bleeding time. Nobody had.

"That's because it's an old test. Older than me, even. I predict the new bullshit computer program doesn't even list it in its test options." With a twinkle in his eye, Fahim ordered the resident to call the hematology lab and ask them to send a veteran technician to perform the test. Turning to Gary, he said, "If her blood pressure doesn't respond to the second unit of blood, start her on a Levophed drip."

He rapped the bedside table with his knuckles, signaling he was finished with the patient, and went on to the next bed, saying, "Let's finish with rounds, I missed breakfast and I'm starving."

Gary watched Mrs. Mudge carefully for the next hour, monitoring her blood pressure and watching for any signs of a possible reaction to the blood transfusion. But the patient showed no fever, rash or drop in blood pressure. He had seen a severe blood reaction once in his nursing career and was not anxious to go through it again.

<><><><><><>

Abrahm returned from his meeting in the sewing room to the dialysis unit, where he immediately began wiping down a reclining chair a patient had just left. He preferred bleach to the other cleaning products because of its power to kill bacteria of all types.

Finishing in the patient treatment area, he went back to the prep room where the techs broke down and repaired the dialysis machines. Dante Soleil was busy replacing the motor on one of the old machines, using parts from an even older device to keep it running.

"Hey, Dante," the housekeeper called. "Can I ask you something?"

Dante looked up. His head was covered with a cap, concealing the dreadlocks he kept out of the way during working hours.

"What's you want with me, mon?" said Dante.

"Do you hear of this paper? It says we should stop the union and have nobody represent us? You hear of such thing?"

Dante shrugged. "Yeah, I saw the petition."

"What do you think?"

"I think it's okay with me. What's the union ever done for me? Nothin'. They got their favorites, same as the bosses. Us Jamaicans get the worst every time. No promotions. Last pick of vacations. Union don't mean shit t' me no how."

Abrahm looked hard at the young man. "Don't you know what is like to work in place where the boss can do you evil all the time and you have no one to stand with you? No one to help you? Without union you are nobody. You are nothing."

"Yeah?" Dante put down the tool and faced Abrahm. Lean and tall, he stared at the Russian. "You tell that Lenny Moss I got no problem signing no petition. The union's no friend a mine. All us Jamaicans feel the same way."

He turned his back and returned to working on the dialysis machine, while Abrahm left, seeing it would do no good to argue further. He needed to find another way to convince the young man of his foolishness. It would take some serious thinking.

<><><><><><>

Roger Slocum held open the door to the administrative conference room and ushered Miss Wiggins and her companion into the room. Before them lay a sumptuous spread of food. The buffet included salmon filets over beds of creamy rice, thickly sliced roast beef with gravy, and barbecued ribs in a thick, sweet sauce. There were roasted vegetables and a lavish salad bar. And to drink, sparkling white wine and imported beer.

"It's just a few things our chef threw together at the last moment. If we'd had more time to plan...Well, the important thing is, you can't work those long hours on the road without a good meal now and again, can you?"

Wiggins allowed a thin smile to lift her sour lips. Quite fond of barbecued ribs, she decided to take an extra long lunch break. With more than one glass of wine.

FIFTEEN

Dr. Auginello stepped into the ICU and greeted Dr. Fahim, who took one look at the lanky Infectious Disease doctor and broke out in laughter.

"What's with the button, Michael?" Fahim asked.

Auginello poked his tongue in his cheek and thought how best to explain the button on his lab coat with the bold letters declaring **SAVE THE STOOL!**

"One of the ID Fellows is doing a study. We've got to do *something* about the epidemic of C. difficile diarrhea going around. It's not just here at James Madison, it's worldwide, you understand."

"It is a frightening infection. Last month I had a transplant patient with colitis that did not respond to any treatment!"

"Those are the toughest cases, all the immune suppressive drugs they're on."

"Precisely. I told the patient he could keep his kidney or keep his colon. He chose to keep the kidney."

"That's what the ID fellow is trying to prevent. She's saving stool samples from high risk patients who are about to be given a course of broad spectrum antibiotics. Her idea is -"

"I understand! After we suppress the patient's normal bowel flora with the antibiotics, you're going to re-seed the colon with the patient's own stool and prevent the C. diff from proliferating. My god, it's *brilliant*!"

"It is a clever idea, I wish I'd come up with it, but it came from my Fellow. She read about a research study done in Sweden."

"They always were anal over there," said Fahim.

"I can't speak to their psychological profile. I can only tell you the Northern Europeans in general are much more advanced than us Americans with regard to infection prevention."

Fahim asked who would be collecting the stools. Auginello told him Pharmacy would text the ID Fellow when a patient with a high risk of developing C. diff diarrhea was about to start a course of broad spectrum antibiotics. The Fellow would perform a rectal exam and save a smear.

Turning to Mrs. Mudge, the patient at hand, Auginello said, "My ID Fellow seems to think Mrs. Mudge is suffering from alcohol withdrawal. There doesn't seem to be strong clinical evidence of an infection. Is that your take?"

"I agree," said Fahim, walking to the patient's bedside. "I am deferring an LP until I see how she does with Librium for withdrawal."

"Good old Librium. Still a good choice for DT's."

"Yes, my friend. Some of the old treatments still have their place." Fahim's eyes twinkled. "You know, Michael, this new computer program for diagnosis and treatment, it is very flawed. It did not recommend Librium. It is programmed to give the latest, most expensive therapies."

"I agree, the program has its limits. But I'm excited to be seeing all the relevant data displayed in one window all at once. I can visualize the x-ray, check the vital signs and review the current meds all at the same time. That's a huge advantage."

"Okay, it will save me some time, not having to jump from program to program. But it cannot substitute the knowledge of an experienced physician!"

"It's not supposed to replace us, it's supposed to help us do our jobs better," said Auginello.

"*Is* it?" Fahim's eyes turned dark and angry. "Do not be so sure, my friend. In other hospitals that Croesus took over, a year after bringing their fancy computer program online, they fired a third of the physicians."

"I don't believe it," said Auginello."

"I will get you the news articles, you can read about it for yourself. Do not be fooled. This program is designed to replace the physician. Your job and mine, they are in danger."

<><><><><><>

Joe West sat beside Miss Burgess, Roger Slocum and Nelson Freely, the director of Human Resources as they reviewed the results of the day's NASH survey. Miss Burgess said the surveyors had found several deficiencies, but nothing that she thought would trigger a failing grade.

"Some of the saline flushes were out of date, but only by a month," she said. "Two nurses couldn't recite the proper response to a fire situation, but the gentleman on the survey understood they were just nervous."

"What about that patient who fell out of bed and fractured her hip?" asked Slocum. "Do they know about the missing neurology consult?"

Burgess assured him the consult had been put in the chart before the surveyors got to it and that all the dates and times were appropriate.

Slocum tapped the desk with his pen and looked at West. "What about the right to work petition? How is that going?"

"I've got followers in dialysis, pharmacy and the research center clericals," said West. "There are divisions between the American born blacks and the foreign born ones that we're exploiting. And Security, of course. My people are one hundred percent behind the decertification."

"Good. If we can dump the union, Croesus is bound to keep all of us in our positions."

West leaned forward. "We need to get rid of Lenny Moss. He's bound to stir up the rabble with his lefty bullshit. I want to terminate him."

Mr. Freely coughed gently, withdrawing a lavender handkerchief from his suit pocket. "Are you sure that's a good idea? Lenny has many friends in this institution, even among some of the front line managers. If you fire him it will raise a great deal of animosity.

Sometimes you catch more flies with honey than you can with vinegar."

"I say you cut off the head of the snake, it writhes for awhile and then it dies," said West. "We have to get rid of Moss. He's too dangerous to keep around."

Burgess agreed with the chief of security, but Slocum admitted termination was risky.

Freely pointed out that the union contract was still in place. "You must have cause to fire an employee, and Lenny is very careful. He never defies a supervisor's orders directly."

"I know all his tricks," said West. "He'll tell his supervisor he's going to the storeroom for supplies, but he makes three stops along the way."

"What if we moved his assigned work area to the grounds outside the hospital?" said Slocum. "That would keep him isolated and alone."

"Good idea," said West. "I can have my security guards keep track of his movements with a video camera. When he goes to an unauthorized area, we'll have photographic proof he violated his work assignment."

Freely tried to object, but he was clearly outnumbered by the others. They were willing to terminate Lenny, whatever it took. Most of all, Freely was deeply troubled by the way they were building their case against Lenny. Having negotiated with the wily shop steward on many occasions, he had grown to respect what the man stood for. There was a right way and a wrong way to impose discipline on a work force. Setting a trap with hidden video cameras was not the right way to go about it.

SIXTEEN

After punching out at the dreaded time clock with the camera mounted above it, Lenny made his way to the hospital benefits office, where he found a languorous blonde with a prodigious diamond ring on her finger, surrounded by stacks of files.

"Hey, Monica. How's Bryan?"

"Don't ask, my husband's gone totally insane." She explained that he had applied to Temple for a program in broadcast journalism. "He's a damn high school music teacher! What does he know about *journalism*?"

"Hey, every man's got to chase his dream."

"So whatever happened to a little house in the country and a bunch of children?"

When Monica asked what she could do for him, he explained he was checking on Louie's death benefits. "In the past some of our member's families haven't gotten their life insurance payment for three, four months. I wanted to see, will there be any problems with this one."

Monica frowned. "I'm not supposed to give out protected information to just anybody, you know."

"Yeah, I know. But the widow is a mess. She's devastated. Matilda doesn't have it together to check on details like this, so she asked me to follow up for her."

"Oh, okay, as long as the widow asked you." Monica called up the program on her computer and identified Louis Gordon. "Yes, here it is. Since he died while still working full time, his family's entitled to one third of his last year's salary." She squinted and looked more closely at the screen. "Hmm. There seems to be a late change to his beneficiary."

"Oh?" Lenny leaned over the desk so he could see the screen, catching a whiff of her lavender perfume. "Who's named in the insurance?"

"It's somebody named Roland Weekes. Is he a relative or something?"

"No, he's not a relative." Lenny felt a bitter chill. If Louie had been in fear for his life, maybe suicide was the only way out he could see, knowing Matilda would go ballistic if she found out that he'd signed his insurance policy to somebody else. While Lenny didn't relish the idea of being the one to tell her, giving her the money he was collecting and withholding the truth about the life insurance seemed like a cruel trick to play. He decided to make a decision when he brought her the money.

"Thanks, Monica. I owe you."

"Anything for you, Lenny. You know that," she said with a bright smile. Married or not, the young woman found something about Lenny that drew her. He wasn't handsome, that was for sure. But he was just so solid a man, and he listened to her; really listened, as if whatever she said was the most important thing in the world to him.

Well, she had a good husband. If she could just knock some sense into his dreamy head.

<><><><><><>

The Medical Examiner completed his gross dissection of the body, with his assistant Harvey weighing each organ as it was removed and slicing slim sections from it for the microscopic examination. The preliminary findings were what he expected. Some liver damage and a thickened heart muscle from years of untreated hypertension. The lungs showed advanced disease, no surprise, but something else was surprising.

"Harvey, take a look at the distal trachea," said the doctor.

His assistant leaned over the table to inspect the organ. "Tight. Very tight," he said. "What's it mean?"

"I'm not sure, yet, Harvey. But the gross anatomy strongly

suggests this man suffered from an asthma attack shortly before he died. Fix me a slide of the tracheal tissue, please."

Harvey placed a slim slice of tissue from the airway on a slide, stained it and placed it under the microscope for his boss to review. The doctor studied the slide, muttering, "Uh-huh. I thought as much. Take a look."

While Harvey looked into the microscope, the doctor explained how the cells had changed their cell wall structure. "It's called remodeling. It happens over many years of reactive disease. This man definitely suffered from asthma."

"You thinking he didn't hang himself after all?"

"I am thinking, Harvey, that this death is awfully suspicious. It seems quite unlikely that someone who is already gasping for breath is going to tie a rope to a pipe and hang himself. Hand me the photos from the scene, please."

The doctor reviewed the photos Harvey had taken of the ligature marks around the neck. It was puzzling. While the marks from the rope were in an upward angle, indicating that the deceased had definitely hung from the rope in a death struggle, the constricted airway suggested an asthma attack caused by some powerful allergen.

Well, the toxicology report should shed light on the cause of death. The ME wished he could obtain the results right away, but the city lab was slow as molasses. He's just have to wait to see what drugs or other allergy-triggering substances were in the blood stream.

A most puzzling case.

After Harvey completed labeling and bagging all the specimens, he helped the doctor sew the body back up so that it would look half way presentable at the funeral. As he sewed, the assistant thought the autopsy findings made an intriguing story that a good friend of his would like very much to hear.

SEVENTEEN

Gary Tuttle kept a close eye on Mrs. Mudge's blood pressure and heart rate as the GI doctor administered the sedative and began the endoscopy. Gently snaking the fiber optic scope down the esophagus, he rotated the illuminated lens back and forth, examining the stomach.

"The damn mucosa looks like raw meat," he muttered. "It's a miracle she didn't bleed out and expire during surgery."

Dr. Fahim stood behind the GI doctor watching the images on the video screen. "I suspected as much," he said, to his team as much as to himself as to the consultant performing the procedure. "All the aspirin the woman has taken eroded the lining of her stomach. It will heal up in a month or so, *if* she avoids ingesting any acids and takes her medications." He stepped back, giving the GI doctor room to pull the scope out and deposit it on the top of the procedure cart.

"Assuming she survives," the GI doctor observed.

"*Why shouldn't she survive?* We can control her bleeding. Tomorrow I will have her extubated and breathing on her own."

Of all Fahim's traits that Gary admired, he thought the doctor's unending optimism was one of the best. Not that Dr. Fahim would argue to prolong a life when all hope was gone. No, he was a strong advocate for withdrawing treatment and administering comfort measures when further treatment was futile. But until he decided the patient was terminal, he never gave up hope.

<><><><><><>

Sitting in the bed beside his stepson Malcolm, Lenny watched as the boy read from his school book. The child ran his finger beneath each word as he read, stumbling over the long words.

"That's great! You're really getting the hang of it."

Tucking the child in and kissing the top of his head, Lenny ambled to the master bedroom, where Patience was rubbing lotion into her dry skin.

"Lenny! Look at the bottom of my feet! *Look*!"

He knelt down, grabbed one leg by the ankle and pulled it up so he could see the sole.

"Feel it!" she said.

He gently ran his finger over the thick callous. "Damn. This is the worst I've ever seen it. You've got to make an appointment with the podiatrist. You can see him when your shift ends."

"I know I should. I just never seem to have the time. With meeting the kids' bus and all the rest..."

"Want me to make the appointment for you?"

"Would you? That'd be great, thanks." She kissed him on the cheek, then settled back into bed, smiling. What would she ever do without her Lenny? She remembered the time he had been so terribly sick, lying in the ICU with the breathing tube in his throat. At the time she had been so relieved to know his friend Gary Tuttle was the nurse, and Crystal cared for him at night.

The thought of losing him had terrified her. But over time, as he healed from his deep injuries and eventually returned to work, her fears subsided.

Lenny looked over, saw her looking at him and smiling.

"What are you smiling about?"

"Oh, nothing important. Nothing worth mentioning."

He took up a book, a history of the Irish famine, and settled back, thinking his wife had a lot of strange fancies, and it was just as well she kept them to herself, he'd never understand them anyway.

EIGHTEEN

With his time card in hand, Lenny stepped up to the time clock and was about to insert it in the hated mechanism when the voice of his Housekeeping supervisor called out, "Yo, Moss! Get your ass in here! Mister Childress wants to see you!"

Punching in, Lenny steeled himself for another piece of bad news as he trudged to the office, where the secretary with skin tight jeans and a low cut top ushered him into the director's office.

The first thing Lenny noticed was that Childress's ash colored hair was cut even shorter than usual. The wily union steward figurerd the bastard was adopting a military look to curry favor with Reichart, the new enforcer for Croesus. The second was the look of contempt on his boss's face; a look even more pronounced than usual.

"Don't bother sitting down, you won't be here that long," said Childress. "You're assigned to a new work area as of today."

"Oh? What is it, Psych?" Most of the housekeeping staff hated to work in the inpatient psychiatric ward. The housekeeping duties were actually quite light, since the doctors didn't undertake a lot of messy procedures or test. Mainly the housekeepers didn't like being locked in the ward along with the patients, and some of the people under treatment were unpredictable. Not often violent, just unpredictable. And scary.

"Not Psych," said Childress. "You're working the grounds. Report to Mister Aleqawa immediately. He'll meet you at the loading dock."

"What's the deal? The grounds keeping was always Henry's assignment."

"Henry's on medical leave. Until he returns you work there. And after he returns, *you work there.*"

Dismissing Lenny with a wave of his hand, Childress looked

down at a paper on his desk as if Lenny had ceased to exit. Lenny realized he had no say in where he was assigned to work. There were seniority issues related to getting a day shift, but the union contract gave management authority to assign workers wherever the saw fit.

Not wasting words on a hopeless argument, Lenny headed for the loading dock, where two trucks were already disgorging their contents of supplies for the kitchen and the supply room. He spotted Aleqawa, a heavyset Middle Eastern man with a pot belly and a bad toupee, standing on the dock.

Aleqawa smiled a toothy smile. "Lenny Moss! The mayor of James Madison. I am so pleased to be working with you. I have heard many many things about you."

The portly man gave Lenny a work sheet with a list of tasks. "Your first duty will be to pick up all of the trash that is littering the grounds and to empty all of the trash receptacles in the loading zone. Then you will proceed to the grounds outside the Emergency Room and repeat the process. *Then* you will repeat the process at the main entrance to the hospital."

The supervisor pointed to a long handled dust pan and broom and a stack of heavy duty trash bags. "When you have finished your first assignment, you will call me at the extension on your work list. I will come and check your work before you go on to the next task. Understood?"

"What about a partner? Henry always worked with a partner."

"Your partner called in sick today. I have no one to replace him. You will carry out your work alone for the time being."

Picking up his tools, Lenny was already framing the grievance he planned to file on his work assignment, anticipating he would be ordered to do the work of two men for a prolonged period. "How much time you gonna give me to finish the first job?"

With a mocking grin, Aleqawa told Lenny the first round of grounds keeping usually took two hours, no more. But because he was working alone *for the day,* he would be given an extra thirty minutes to get it all done.

Lenny cursed under his breath, not bothering to inform the bastard about his plans for filing a complaint. Better to let the unfair practice continue a while until he had enough evidence to grieve it.

He began sweeping up the debris that had accumulated in the loading area during the night. The May sun was warm and the air humid with the threat of rain. It was going to be a long day.

<><><><><><>

Dr. Fahim stood with his arms crossed over his chest, frowning. The report on Mrs. Mudge from the resident who covered nights was not good. In fact, it was terrible.

"Tell me her lactate level," Fahim said as he observed the woman's mouth making gasping movements like a fish out of water, even though a ventilator was supporting her breathing with a high percentage oxygen delivered directly into her lungs.

"The lactate is six point three," said the resident.

"She is in septic shock. You gave her three units of blood and her hemoglobin is still not back to normal. I am certain she is bleeding into her GI tract. Quite possibly into her hip as well."

"Her coags are just about back to baseline, but her bleeding time is still abnormal," said the resident.

"Give two more units of blood," said Fahim. "We must stop the bleeding."

As the resident made out the requests for blood, he asked Dr. Fahim how long could they go on giving the patient blood products.

"All bleeding stops eventually," said Fahim, leaving his team to ponder the two possible outcomes for a GI bleed: it stops, or the patient dies. "And call the Infectious Disease service. With the denuded lining of her stomach she is a prime candidate for a blood infection. We must find it and treat it, or you will be observing an autopsy instead of asking rehab to instruct her how to walk on her repaired hip."

Dr. Fahim was about to go on to the next ICU patient when he spied an unwanted trio coming in through the automatic doors.

"Oh my god," mumbled Fahim. "This is not what I need just when we're half way through morning rounds."

The team turned to see what had interrupted their Attending's morning routine, which was as sacred as any ancient text. The Fellow asked Fahim, "Who are those people?"

Fahim shook his head sadly.

"They are the NASH surveyors, accompanied by the Director of Nursing. And I am one hundred percent certain they are going to ask about our septic, bleeding and coagulopathic Miss Mudge.

NINETEEN

Once the NASH team entered the ICU accompanied by Miss Burgess, the head of housekeeping and the chief engineer, Miss Wiggins demanded to see the chart for Mrs. Mudge. When Gary Tuttle retrieved the chart and handed it to her, the surveyor informed him they were conducting a continuity of care survey. She asked what had been in the report that the Recovery Room nurse gave the nurse. While Gary showed her the written transfer report, Wiggins scrutinized the document carefully.

"I don't see in the Recovery nurse's report anything about a history of aspirin abuse. Don't you think that would be an important element to include in the transfer report?"

"She told me about the aspirin, it's in my note," said Gary. He pointed in the chart where he had written a brief summary of the patient's condition and the main events that led to the surgery. "See? I wrote about the possible bleeding disorder due to alcohol and or aspirin."

Apparently mollified, Miss Wiggins went on to interview Dr. Fahim. She asked him if he was confident that the surgeon had known about the patient's prior aspirin and alcohol abuse before beginning the operation on her hip.

"Of course he knew. He must have known," said Fahim. "Why do you doubt that he knew all her history?"

"Because he and the anesthesiologist made no mention of the risk of her aspirin use or her alcohol intake in any of their notes."

"You must ask the surgeon what he was aware of, I cannot read his mind. I can only tell you that when I consulted on the patient last night I knew clearly that she had significant risks for post-operative bleeding, and I took all necessary measures to minimize that risk."

"Yes, I see that, your note is quite clear. You list the aspirin and the alcohol. You also list her age as a risk of infection."

"Immuno-senesnce. I am afraid that as we grow older, our immune system grows weaker. It is the price we pay for our longevity."

Wiggins pulled her glasses up over her forehead and studied one entry in the ICU consultation note. "I see you ordered a bleeding time test. I haven't seen that test done in years. Decades, even. Don't you have more advanced, more accurate tests for coagulation available?"

Fahim chuckled, his eyes sparkling with amusement. "Sometimes the old ways are still the best. Don't you agree?"

Wiggins looked skeptical but decided not to challenge the Attending physician in charge of the ICU.

Having stood holding her breath and praying the NASH team did not find proof that the surgeon had blundered into the operation without knowing the patient's medical history, Miss Burgess tried to distract the surveyor by pointing out the new advanced computerized diagnostic program. She explained how the system tracked the patient's vital signs, lab results, medications and even diagnostic tests in real time.

"It sends alerts to the clinician whenever there's a potential conflict between medication and disorder," she said.

"Did it send an alert about the potential bleeding disorder to the orthopedic surgeon before the operation?" Wiggins asked.

"Uh, no, we have not yet incorporated the consultation note into the computerized database. But that's coming in the next quarter!"

Wiggins cast a skeptical glance at the nursing director and moved on to another patient.

<><><><><><>

Mimi was mixing her morning IV medications. Wearing disposable gloves and a surgical mask, she carefully injected an antibiotic into a fifty cc bag, then peeled off a label from the medication vial and slapped it onto the bag.

She had just started on her fourth medication when she saw the nursing supervisor coming toward her; always a bad sign. Why couldn't the supervisors ever come with good news? Why couldn't they give her something to make their work easier?

"Mimi," said the supervisor. "I have a messaging unit for you." The woman reached into her bag and came up with a small, black device on a thick, lavender string. "You will wear this around your neck at all times. The call center will inform you when a patient under your care requires assistance."

"I heard about this. They're replacing the call lights outside the rooms, aren't they?"

"Not replacing. *Augmenting*. Our studies have shown that the time nursing takes to answer patient requests is entirely too long. We average over *eight point five minutes* to respond to the patient. It's no wonder our patient satisfaction surveys are in the toilet."

Mimi recalled the memo that Miss Burgess had sent out the week before describing the new system. An operator, *not* a nurse, would be responding to patients who press their call button. The operator would ask what the patient needed and would then call the nurse and tell her what she needed to do.

"You will wear this throughout your shift. When the device chimes you will place the ear piece in your ear and hear the instruction. You will then proceed immediately to fulfill your patient's request."

Not remaining to answer any questions, the supervisor went off to distribute the rest of her 'messaging devices.' Mimi realized the woman had not bothered to mention that the device had a GPS unit that tracked where the nurse was every minute of her shift. Supposedly, this was going to help the call operator find the nurse closest to the patient. The memo that explained the system hadn't mentioned that the system was also going to track *where every nurse was every minute of the shift,* as well as how much time the nurse took to meet the patient's request. If the nurse took too long to satisfy the patient's needs, she would be written up. Termination would be the inevitable result of a slow response.

Sighing, Mimi slung the device around her neck, put the ear bud in her ear, and pushed her cart onto the ward. She looked up and down the corridor for Lenny, thinking she would cry a little on his shoulder, he was always such a good listener. She walked toward the housekeeping closet at the end of the hall, where Little Mary was stocking her cart.

"Where's Lenny?" Mimi asked.

Mary's face tightened with anger. Stuffing another roll of toilet paper into her cart, she said, "They done pulled Lenny out a' the hospital and moved him to the grounds. He ain't in the hospital no more."

TWENTY

Lenny was sweeping up debris along the curb at the main entrance when he spotted an old security guard rolling toward him on a little electric cart. The guard stopped the vehicle and slowly eased his way out of the seat.

"Lenny Moss. Looks like Joe West decided you needed more fresh air and sunshine."

"Hi, Sandy. Yeah, I'm really enjoying the air. Did you know the number twenty-three buses on Germantown Ave use clean technology? I kind of miss that black soot they used to belch when they pull out into traffic."

Sandy chuckled. "You should be wearin' a hat, though. Don't want that bald spot on the back a' your head gettin' burned none."

"Gee, thanks, I'll pick something up at the Dollar Store soon as my shift ends." Lenny returned to sweeping the trash. "How's the back doing? You seem to be moving a little better this morning."

"Yeah, man, I got me one of them injections. The doc shot me up right in the spine. Doin' a world of good."

Lenny asked how it looked for the security department signing the decertification petitions. Sandy told him he was likely the only guard refusing to sign it; that Joe West had everybody running scared.

"You think they'll get enough votes to kick out the union?"

"Honestly, we've just begun to fight it, it's too early to tell. I know a lot of workers are pissed at Croesus. But there are plenty who are unhappy with the union, too, so how it turns out..."

"I'm waiting to hear when the union will hold a meeting. That should be a hell of an event."

The old guard had sagging jowls like a pug and watery eyes. He lifted his security cap and scratched his shaved head. "Looks like Joe West is gonna keep you out here a long old time. Keep you from makin' trouble."

"Yeah, I expect he'll keep me on the grounds detail until he fires my ass."

"Prob'bly so," said Sandy, nodding his head. Then the old guard climbed back onto his electric cart, leaving Lenny to continue with his labors. Neither man noticed the big, burly security guard standing inside the hospital entrance with the camera. The man had been videotaping Lenny's encounter with Sandy, using a telephoto lens to capture their every movement.

Though the burly guard stopped recording, he continued to watch Lenny at work, as he had done from the moment the man had arrived at his new assignment.

<><><><><><>

For the second time that morning the Medical Examiner reviewed the copy of Louis Gordon's medical records that the James Madison Employee Health nurse had faxed to him. The information confirmed his suspicions: the man had been experiencing asthma for years. There was little doubt the victim had suffered an acute attack at the time of his demise; the edema and inflammation in the soft tissue were classic signs of status asthmaticus, an asthma attack that does not respond to treatment.

Harvey asked him why didn't the victim get treatment for his attack.

"Also something I've puzzled over." The doctor instructed Harvey to search the clothes that the deceased had been wearing for an inhaler for asthma. Searching the pockets, Harvey pulled a small, round object from the pants. It was an inhaler.

"Just as I suspected," said the ME. "Let me see it."

Receiving the inhaler, the doctor turned the opening of the inhaler away from his face and pressed firmly on the trigger, releasing a robust spray of medication.

The doctor looked at Harvey, who shrugged his shoulders.

"Makes you wonder why he didn't get relief from his asthma, doesn't it?"

"It does indeed," said the doctor. "The question that comes to my mind is, was his asthma attack refractory to his medication?"

"A really bad attack, you mean," said Harvey.

"That's right. But the problem *that* raises is, the man worked in a *hospital*. If you were suffering an attack and your medication gave you no relief, where is the first place you would visit?"

"The Emergency Room."

"The Emergency Room." The doctor put the inhaler down on the table and stared at it. He wanted more than anything to know if someone had prevented the victim from using it. Because if they did, that was clearly a case of manslaughter.

Wondering what other surprises they were going to find, the ME told Harvey he wished they'd received a preliminary toxicology report.

"I got it," said Harvey. Seeing the look of surprise on his boss's face, he explained that he'd called over yesterday and told a buddy they had a homicide case and needed to get the results right away. Harvey pulled the report from the fax machine and handed it to the doctor.

"Amazing. The city lab never works this fast."

"Nothin' like havin' friends," said Harvey, looking at the report over his boss's shoulder.

The doctor scanned the lab results, noting the abnormalities. "Marijuana, no surprise. Sugar elevated, he probably didn't take care of his diabetes, either." Suddenly he stabbed the paper with his finger. "Christ! Harvey, look at this!"

He pointed at another finding, cursing again under his breath. "Strychnine. In the goddamned blood and lung tissue. He must have inhaled it with his marijuana. Jesus H. Christ, no wonder he had a fatal asthma attack...*Strychnine*."

Harvey took the report from the doctor's hand and laid it on his boss's desk. He was used to hearing reports of poisons in a victim's blood. But this was the first time he'd come across strychnine.

"Somebody wanted this guy stone cold dead, didn't he?" said Harvey,

"There's no doubt this time," said the doctor. "The deceased obviously indulged in his marijuana habit. By itself, not a complete surprise, addicted people feed their addiction even when it exacerbates an underlying chronic disease. But the strychnine is not something our dead friend chose to ingest. Without a doubt he was the victim of foul play."

The doctor picked up the phone and dialed the police precinct that covered James Madison Hospital. When an officer answered, the doctor said, "This is the Medical Examiner's office. I need to speak with Detective Joseph Williams."

While the ME was talking with Detective Williams, Harvey sent a text message to a friend at James Madison hospital who was in the same line of work. A friend who would be highly interested in the autopsy report so far. His buddy Regis Devoe was going to buy him more than one round of drinks when he found out what kind of shit the ME was uncovering. And Harvey was determined to order the best whiskey in the joint.

<><><><><><>

Responding to his request for a consultation, Dr. Auginello approached Fahim, who was in his tiny vestibule in the ICU writing his notes. "Hey, Samir. I see Mudge's lactate is trending up."

"Yes, it is alarming." He turned in his chair to speak to his friend. "We are giving bicarb for the acidosis and the broad spectrum antibiotics as you suggested." Fahim stood up and rubbed his belly, having missed breakfast, his favorite meal. "At least she has a chance to survive. "Not like that poor fellow we coded who hung himself the other day."

"You were at that code?"

"I was there at the end, my resident called me. They were having trouble bagging the patient. His airway was completely occluded."

"That was from the noose compressing his trachea, don't you think? It must have caused massive edema in the soft tissue."

Fahim shrugged. "Maybe so, maybe not." Seeing a quizzical look on Auginello's face, Fahim went on to explain that a compression fracture from a noose would of course constrict the airway. But once the noose was removed, the positive pressure from a bag mask blowing into the airway should have expanded the collapsed trachea.

"Was there blood in the airway that clotted?" said Auginello, poking his tongue in his cheek and considering different scenarios.

Fahim shook his head, "I believe there is more going on here than a manual strangulation. We must wait for the Medical Examiner's report. Then we will know if the worst has happened."

"The worst?" said Auginello. "You mean..."

"I mean murder. We must wait for the report from the Medical Examiner. Then we will know if our lowly dialysis technician died by his own sorrowful hand, or if his life was taken from him against his will."

TWENTY-ONE

After depositing the trash in a dumpster, Lenny called the office and told them he was going for lunch. He picked up a cup of coffee and a sandwich from a food cart on the sidewalk and made his way to the sewing room, where he found Moose, Birdie and Little Mary already waiting for him.

"Lenny!" Moose called as soon as his friend was through the door. "You think this decert campaign's gonna get anywhere?"

"I say it sinks like a turd in a toilet," said Mary.

"Thank you for the colorful metaphor," Lenny said, unfolding a chair and settling down. "We can't take anything for granted." When Moose and Mary protested in unison, Lenny said, "We can't underestimate the ability of the bosses to pull the wool over some people's eyes."

"Lenny's right," said Birdie, snipping a thread from a newly repaired gown and folding it neatly. "We got some fools in this hospital would vote against their own mother."

Little Mary held a fat business envelope in her hand, saying, "I got a couple more people to talk to. I'll give you all the money I collected for Louie soon's I get done. Okay?"

"That's fine," said Lenny. After suggesting they try to finish the fund-raising by Saturday morning, he filled them in on what he knew about a decertification campaign.

Little Mary's face contorted with anger. "'Member all them folks who spoke against the union at the last meeting? That time when we warned about Croesus buying up the hospital? A lotta the brothers and sisters don't trust the union no how."

Moose said, "I can't believe anybody's gonna believe all the bullshit the company's putting out about 'righting the ship' and bringing in a bunch a' new patients with big bucks. I just can't."

Lenny said, "Don't underestimate the silver tongue those

bastards have. Croesus is telling the rank and file that *we're* the problem. That if they can take a free hand organizing a 'flexible' work force, they'll turn James Madison into an efficient, *profit-making* facility."

"Yeah, they gonna make a pile a' money," said Little Mary. "But they makin' it for *them,* not for us. We ain't gonna see nothin' but more work and less pay. Hell, I can barely make it through the month, the little itty-bitty money they puts in *my* paycheck."

"All of which will come *if* they can decertify the union," said Lenny. "For the moment they're saying they will freeze our benefit costs and retirement package for eighteen months and not lay off any workers, *if the decert election goes their way.*"

"After that there's gonna be cuts. And lots of 'em," said Moose. "So when's the union holding the meeting?"

"The area rep put in the request, we're waiting to get the approval for the auditorium, it's the only place big enough to hold everybody. In the meantime we have to write that flyer and give it out. Can you guys meet me at the Cave tonight at, say, six and help draft it?"

Moose and Birdie volunteered, but Little Mary kept quiet. When Lenny gave her a questioning look, Mary said, "Come on, Lenny. You know I don't write all that good. You got all the words we need."

"Sure, I can spin a whole bunch of bullshit and it will sound good, but you've got the anger and the experience that we need to really make our case as strong as we can."

"I don't know..."

"Hey, every time there's an attack on one of the workers, you're out there running your mouth, telling it like it is. You have all the words we need, Mary."

The housekeeper looked down at the ground, embarrassed at the praise. But secretly she was pleased that Lenny appreciated her place in the fight. She wanted nothing more than to take a poke at one of the bosses.

“Yeah, all right, I’ll meet you. But you buyin’ the drinks!”

“Buying you a drink will be my pleasure,” said Lenny. “Just don’t ask me to match you shot for shot, I know you can drink me under the table any time.”

“You an’ every other man in this rat hole of a hospital.” Mary rose and marched out of the room, saying she’d see them at the bar at six o’clock, and they better not be late or she’d whup their ass in front of everybody.

<><><><><><>

On his way back to his work area, Lenny passed by the outpatient suites. Seeing the secretary for orthopedics was free, he stopped in and asked for an appointment for his wife with the podiatrist.

“Hi, Lenny,” said the secretary, a pudgy Latina woman with a gold necklace, a lavender shawl and matching lavender earrings.

“You’re looking sharp today,” he said, noting the matching outfit.

“Why thank you, Lenny. Give me a mo’, let me check the computer for an opening.”

It took a few minutes for her to get the proper screen up and running. Finally she found an open date and filled out an appointment card. Handing Lenny the card, she added, “Any services we can offer you? No trouble with your knees or hips? All recovered from your injuries?”

“Yes, I’m fully recovered, thank you.”

“Well don’t be a stranger, we’re open every day ‘til closing. Except weekends. And holidays.”

Promising to stay in touch, Lenny made his way back to his work area outside the hospital’s main entrance. Taking up his broom and long-handled dustpan, he didn’t notice the burly security guard stationed in an unmarked car in the parking lot watching him. Nor could he know that Joe West was standing in the control room of the security office watching the entrance to the hospital on the remote cameras. The cameras did not show every single square foot of the hospital. but they covered enough ground to show Lenny going downstairs to the sewing room, and then stopping at the orthopedic clinic before returning to his work area.

West wrote down the times stamped on the camera. His shark eyes glistened, seeing that Lenny had gone a full fifteen minutes over his allotted break time. It was the second time the steward had been out of his work area without authorization. The infractions weren't egregious enough to allow West to fire him *that day*, but it was just a matter of time before he had enough infractions to remove the pesky shop steward, permanently.

TWENTY-TWO

Lenny had finished picking up the trash around the loading dock and outside the Emergency Room and was sweeping up debris from the sidewalk in front of the main entrance when he saw Regis Devoe coming toward him.

"Yo, Lenny! What's goin' on?"

Lenny finished scooping some trash into a heavy duty bag and tied it off. "They got me working the grounds. Childress probably thinks I can cause less trouble stuck out here."

"He ain't far from the truth," said Regis. "How *are* you gonna stay in touch with everybody?"

"Simple. I'm going to let you and Moose and the others handle more of the organizing." Lenny looked around; saw a burly security guard standing by the main doors watching them. "Listen, you better get back inside. You don't have an excuse to be out here."

"Yeah, I'm cool, I told Doc Fingers I was goin' outside for coffee. But what I really got is big news. It's about Louie."

"Oh? What?"

"The ME don't think he killed his self. He thinks the man was murdered." Regis told him how Louie had suffered an asthma attack at the time of his death and that it made no sense for a man suffering from asthma tying a rope around his neck and hanging himself. "He'd be too busy trying to catch his breath."

Lenny slowly nodded his head in recognition. "You know, this puts his last message to me in a whole new light. I'm no expert in the psych department, but Louie didn't seem like the kind to do himself in. If he was 'getting out,' he might have meant getting out of the drug business."

"That could be why he signed his life insurance over to his dealer. He was tryin' to settle his debts."

"Could be," said Lenny. "It makes sense."

Regis added the findings of strychnine in the blood, which strengthened the case for murder.

"Christ, wouldn't you know it," said Lenny. "Now I have *another* can of worms to deal with."

"You mean *we* have. You forget me n' Moose and the rest'll help. We in this together."

Lenny agreed, feeling some degree of relief. The cautionary words his wife and friends had been telling him for years was finally sinking in. He couldn't take on all the troubles of the world by himself; he had to rely on his co-workers to carry the weight. It was the only way to survive. The only way to win.

Lenny watched his friend skip up the steps and enter the building, feeling a sense of pride to have such good friends, and not paying attention to the big, beefy security guard posted at the main entrance and watching his every move.

<><><><><><>

Mimi had just sunk into a chair in the charting room behind the station and pulled off her shoes to try and ease the aching in her feet when she heard the voice of the dispatcher speaking in her ear saying patient so-and-so needed a nurse right away. Was this the hundredth time that day the dispatcher had called her? The ear bud was almost as annoying as the voice giving her orders. Mimi knew that the computer system was tracking how long it took her to answer each patient request. But since she was assigned to fifty percent more patients than she had been before Croesus took over, the beleaguered nurse was constantly on her feet running from room to room.

She complained to another nurse sitting beside her that she was going to end up in a hospital bed or the psych unit if they didn't give her *some* time to rest her feet.

She put her shoes back on and trudged to the patient's bedside, where an elderly man complained no one had emptied his potty chair and the smell was making him sick. With a sigh, Mimi put on a plastic apron and gloves and took the bucket beneath the chair into the bathroom, where she hosed the contents into the toilet and rinsed the bucket.

As she was returning the clean bucket to the potty chair, Dr. Auginello came into the room to see how the patient was doing. Mimi reported that the stool was no longer watery and not quite as malodorous, a statement the patient challenged.

"Any word on us using the Dakins solution to bathe the C diff patients like this one?" she asked.

The ID physician told her he had reviewed what little literature there was on the subject, and that he would propose a bathing protocol to the patient's primary physician. "As long as the Attending goes along with it, I see no reason why we can't begin right away."

Pleased that the nurses would finally be doing something to beat back the C. diff bacteria that was causing so much diarrhea in the hospital, Mimi left the patient's room with a broad smile on her face. Until she almost bumped into Miss Orzo, her nursing supervisor. The supervisor pulled out a computer printout and held it out for Mimi to see. "Our time log shows that you have been exceedingly slow in answering your patient's call bells. You're averaging six and a half minutes. That does not meet our Superlative Patient Service initiative. You *must* do better or there will be consequences."

"But Miss Orzo, I'm moving as fast as I can. It's just my patient load is almost double what it was a year ago. How am I gonna meet all their needs? I'm only one little person."

"Our staffing program ensures that you have an adequate number of personnel to meet your patient's needs. There is no shortage of staff, it's simply a matter of effective time management. You must use your time wisely and efficiently."

"That's all well and good, but my feet don't feel very wise. *Or* efficient."

The supervisor took out a form that listed the number of

patients, each ranked by their severity of illness. "You see this number? That is the total number of patient care units for your ward. And *this* number is your staffing level. You can see that your staffing value is exactly equal to your patient care requirements. There should be no delay whatsoever in rendering care to your patients."

Mimi stared at the paper trying to understand it. The numbers all added up, she could see that. But there was something weird about the whole system. Suddenly, the flaw in the staffing system jumped out at her.

"Miss Orzo! Look at your system. You rate an RN and an aide as equal in value. You rate a clerk the same as a nurse, too. That makes no sense to me."

"Oh, are you saying a nurse is a more valued member of the team?"

"It's not that, no, of course not. But an aide can't give out medications. An aide can't check doctor's orders. An aide can't redress a wound or do a physical assessment of a post-op patient."

"All nursing responsibilities, of course."

"But according to your system, we could manage just fine with *one* nurse and like, ten clerks and aides. That's nuts!"

The supervisor closed her folder, removing the staffing paper from Mimi's eyes. "It is not wise, Nurse Thomas, to disparage the carefully thought out, proven methodology of the Croesus system of patient care. This program was designed by *experts.* You will not help yourself by blaming externalities for your professional failures. *Especially* when they involve the serious injury to one of your patients."

"Oh my god, am I really in that much trouble over Mrs. Mudge's fall?"

"You will have to wait for the case review. After that we shall see if your employment at James Madison can continue."

With that the supervisor turned on her heels and walked briskly away. Mimi watched her go in amazement. She had heard a lot of bureaucratic bullshit in her years at James Madison Hospital, but she had never heard such a bald-faced lie in her life.

She decided she needed to go to *somebody* for advice. She knew who that somebody was. The problem was, another custodian was working on her floor. Spotting Little Mary coming down the hall with her housekeeping cart, Mimi called out, "Yo, Mary. Now that Lenny's working outside the hospital, where the heck can I find him?"

TWENTY-THREE

Little Mary dropped herself into the booth beside Lenny, pulled an envelope stuffed with cash from her bag and laid it down in front of Lenny. "Here ya go, that's all I could get for poor Louie."

Lenny's mouth dropped open in amazement at the thick wad of cash. "I don't know how you do it, Mary. I swear, you have a gift. You're the best fund-raiser I've ever worked with."

"Ain't no big thing. You just go up to a worker, grab him by the shirt and tell him you collecting for the widow of one a' our own, and they better come up with some serious green or you'll whup their ass."

"I don't think that approach is going to work for me," said Lenny, laughing.

Moose and Regis each handed Lenny a slimmer envelope with money. Lenny added it to the prodigious amount he had already collected and tucked it all deep inside his knapsack.

"Okay, I'll take the money over to Louie's wife over the weekend. I got a sympathy card and all." He picked up his glass of Irish whiskey for a toast. "To Louie!"

"To Louie!" the others joined in, clinking their glasses and taking a long draft. Mary emptied her double shot of Jack Daniels, wiped her mouth and sat back, at peace.

After a moment of silence, Regis asked when was the union holding the meeting.

"The hospital won't give us a room, the bastards." Lenny explained that when the area representative called the administration to schedule a general meeting in the big auditorium, he was told the room was booked up for the entire month. The best they could give him was a classroom in the medical school.

"How many can you get in a classroom?" asked Birdie.

"Thirty. Maybe thirty-five."

"That's bullshit!" said Regis. "They don't want us to meet!"

"Naturally. I told the rep we should take over the cafeteria at lunch time and call a meeting. But he said they would have grounds for disciplining everyone who attended. Plus, he wouldn't be allowed in the building. So he's going to hold the meeting on Saturday afternoon down the union hall."

Lenny's face turned serious. He took out a legal sized pad and asked, "Okay, let's do it. Tell me why should any of the workers vote to keep the union? What's in it for them?"

"That's easy," said Birdie. "We lose the union, there's more money taken out our pay for health insurance."

"More co-pays for our prescriptions," Little Mary added.

"More part time workers with no benefits," Regis said. "And no job protection." Lenny scribbled notes as Regis added, "With the union they can't up and fire you without a reason."

"And you have the right to appeal it if they write you up and discipline you," Moose added.

"Okay, we have some degree of job security," said Lenny, underlining his note. "What else?"

"Seniority. For getting holidays off, things like that," said Regis. "And for getting assigned the day shift. You work long enough, you should have something for it."

"Okay, seniority." Lenny wrote it on the pad.

"Hey, Lenny," said Mary. "You're so good, writing the flyers and analyzing things, how come you didn't finish up at college?"

Lenny looked at Mary as if she had asked him to strip naked in front of them. "Mary, how do *you* know about my college experience, that was years ago?"

"A little bird sang tweet, tweet, tweet. Now answer my question. When you gonna get your degree?"

"I don't have time for that right now, we're involved in a struggle to save the union."

Moose jabbed Lenny in the arm. "You could've been takin' courses before this shit came down. Mary's right. Why don't you go back to school, get the degree and do something else?"

"Like what?"

"Hell, you could do anything you want," said Mary. "You could be president of the union!"

"That ain't gonna happen," said Lenny. He suggested they discuss his future plans another day and get back to writing the leaflet.

"What we have so far is good, as far as it goes. But I don't think it's not enough to be sure we win the vote. We need something more."

"What about health n' safety?" asked Moose. "You know they gonna ignore all them protections we got now, n' there won't be no union safety officer to investigate unsafe working conditions."

"What you bet, come next flu season Croesus is gonna make us pay for our annual flu shots," said Birdie. "I need that shot, I take medicine for lupus. I can't take a chance with influenza!"

"This is great stuff!" said Lenny, scribbling madly. "The union can find me instances of facilities where they lost the union and safety standards went to hell." He quickly sketched the elements of a flyer, then held it up, asking the others what they thought of it.

Birdie pulled her head back when she saw it. "I don't know, Lenny. I mean, it's kinda strong, isn't it?" She pointed to the line: WANTED: FOR ATTEMPTED MURDER OF THE UNION: ROBERT '3RD RIECH' REICHART

"I guess it is," said Lenny. "But it's fair, don't you think? It fits him, doesn't it?"

Regis liked the slogan, Moose had mixed feelings about it. Seeing that Little Mary was noncommittal, Lenny was about to ask her what bothered her about the flyer when he realized the woman might not know what the Third Reich reference was all about.

Turning to Birdie, Lenny said, "I know linking Reichart with the German Nazi party from World War Two is strong language, but if we mean what we say about how much his policies are killing workers and patients, we should say it like it is, don't you think?"

Little Mary brightened. "It's good. Yeah, it's good, let's use it." The rest of the group agreed, though they were worried about how the administration would respond to it.

Just then Mimi came into the Cave. Moose pulled up an extra chair for her as the nurse apologized for barging in on them uninvited. "Mary told me you'd be here. I hope you don't mind, Lenny, but I need to talk to you, things are getting bad on the ward. Really bad."

"That's just what we were talking about." He asked what she was drinking and ordered a Jack Daniels on the rocks, then he filled her in on their discussion so far and read off the issues they had identified.

Mimi suggested they focus more on how breaking the union will hurt patient care. "Look at us nurses. We've got no union and they're near doubling our patient assignment. *Then,* they have the nerve to discipline us for being late answering a patient call button!"

"She's right," said Moose. "We got to talk about how it'll hurt the patient. Less workers means less care, means more patients ending up *dead*."

Regis drained his glass, set it down on the table and turned to Lenny. "Speaking of dead, did you tell them about what a friend o' mine at the Medical Examiner's said about Louie?"

"No," said Lenny. "I was gonna bring it up after we got the flyer finished."

Everyone wanted to know what Regis was talking about, so he repeated what he learned, that Louie had ingested strychnine with his marijuana and the poison had set off an asthma attack. "My friend in the Medical Examiner's says it don't make sense a man's gonna tie a rope to a pipe and hang himself when he's struggling to take in a breath."

"Somebody done killed poor Louie!" said Mary. "You know what *that* means," she added, poking Lenny in the ribs with her elbow.

"Don't start, Mary. I've got enough shit on my plate. I don't need to take on a murder investigation, too."

"It don't fall just on you!" cried Mary. "We all in it together!"

"I never did believe poor Louie killed himself," said Birdie, her face taught with anger. "He was too much in love with his wife. Wasn't no way he was ever gonna leave her. Not even by dying!"

Lenny told them about Louie signing his life insurance over to his dealer, Ronald Weekes, who drove a car service near the hospital.

"Matilda is gonna go ballistic when she finds out!" said Regis. "She's gonna go to the morgue and stab him in the heart, even though he's dead already."

Everyone agreed, Louie must have been in deep trouble over drugs to stiff his wife on his life insurance. Little Mary suggested that even in heaven, or hell, Louie would still be afraid of his wife's anger over the double cross he pulled.

Lenny called for a second round of drinks. He needed another whiskey, the idea that he would have to investigate Louie's death, even with the help of his friends, was deeply troubling. The fight to save the union was already promising to take up all his time and energy.

Once the new drinks were served, Lenny stirred his with the little straw and then took a long swallow. Seeing his friend was troubled, Moose playfully patted Lenny on the shoulder. "Don't you worry 'bout nothin'," he said. "We'll deal with it. All a' us. Together."

Lenny slowly nodded his head, trying to adjust to the new approach his friends had been urging on him for a long time. "Yeah, I get that. But it's still gonna be a big mess. Once you begin turning over rocks looking for snakes, all kinds of shit comes to light."

"That doesn't hurt us," said Regis. "It hurts the bosses. You gotta believe it wasn't no worker killed Louie. Right?"

"Maybe you're right," said Lenny.

"Trust me. We look into Louie's death, we get more dirt on

somebody high up on the food chain. It's gonna help us."

"I sure hope so," said Lenny. He turned to Mimi and asked what troubles had brought her to the Cave.

"Oh, Lenny. You remember when Mrs. Mudge fell out of bed and broke her hip?" Lenny nodded his head. "Well after she went for surgery to repair the hip she deteriorated, and now she's in the ICU, and she's doing very bad."

"And the bosses are blaming you."

"Of course. The thing is, she was confused when I found her on the floor, but before that she was always sharp as a tack."

"She had a sharp tongue all right," said Lenny.

"Maybe she hit her head," said Regis.

"No, there were no bruises on her head. Just her hip."

"So why was she confused. That's the thing bothering you," Lenny said.

"That's it. If I could find out what made her confused, I could say *that* was what sent her over the side rails."

Lenny considered the issue. "This sounds like a medical question. I think you need to talk to one of the doctors."

"Yeah, I guess so. But you'll defend me if they fire me, won't you? You did such a good job with Paulina. That was amazing, what you did in her hearing."

"It wasn't really all that complicated. But sure, I'll be happy to stand with you if it comes to that. Let me know what you find out."

Having worked a twelve hour shift, Mimi finished her drink and bid them good night. Lenny followed a short time later. As much as he wanted to hang with Mary and the others and keep on drinking, he knew the days ahead would require him to be awake and alert and ready to do battle.

<><><><><><>

While Lenny and his friends were in the Cave discussing their problems, Joe West was in his security control room going over all the tapes of Lenny on the job. They included clandestine video taken by his undercover guard, as well as scenes taken by the regular surveillance cameras placed at strategic locations throughout the hospital.

Alone in the office, West poured himself a glass of scotch and sipped it, neat. His thin lips curled in a satisfied smile. There was enough evidence against the wily steward to put him on probation for a week. It wasn't enough evidence for a termination. Yet. But it would be soon enough. A few more days, a few more infractions on tape, and it would be good-bye, Lenny Moss.

TWENTY-FOUR

After punching in at the time clock, Lenny went to his locker and considered his options. His backpack was filled with the flyer accusing the hospital management of undermining the safety and health of the workers, as well as that of the patients they served. He didn't trust leaving the flyers in his locker, Joe West could inspect it at any time. And he couldn't keep his backpack with him all day, it would be too suspicious.

"Lennye Moss! How are you?"

Lenny turned to see his friend Abrahm seated on a bench putting on his work shoes. "Hey, Abrahm. I'm doing okay, thanks."

Lenny sat down on the bench and looked around the locker room. While there were apparently no video cameras in the area, something the union had argued for and won, he suspected Joe West kept hidden microphones in the area, the bastard was capable of anything.

In a low whisper, Lenny explained his dilemma to Abrahm. The cheerful Russian clapped Lenny on the back, happy to help hide the union flyers. "Count on me, my friend," he whispered. "I will keep the papers in my work area. No one will see them."

They made a plan for Abrahm to stow the flyers in a storage area in the dialysis unit. Regis and Moose would come by, collect bundles of them, and distribute them as they made their rounds.

Lenny left grateful to have such reliable friends to carry out the work.

<><><><><><>

Dr. Fahim pointed at the x-ray on the computer screen and cursed. The other members of his team stared in wonder, having never seen a film as bad as Mrs. Mudge's.

"I don't see why the woman is even alive," said the Fellow, noting the total whiteout of all of the lung fields. Normally the lungs showed black, offering no resistance to the x-rays passing through them. But Mudge's lungs were so congested and inflamed, they blocked the x-rays as if the lungs were packed with cement.

"What is the oxygen concentration?" asked Fahim.

"She's on one hundred percent," said the on-call resident who had covered the previous night. "And twelve of PEEP."

"It is a wonder she did not blow a hole in her lungs with pressure that high," said the Fellow. "It's too bad we can't give her a *higher* concentration of oxygen, but you can't go higher than a hundred percent."

"Actually, you can," said Fahim, with a twinkle in his eyes. He reminded them that putting a patient in a hyperbaric chamber allowed them to increase the partial pressure of oxygen, which, for all intents and purposes, was as good as delivering more than one hundred percent oxygen, since the cells were hyper-saturated from the high pressure.

"The hospital still has a hyperbaric pressure chamber, but it is not set up for someone on a ventilator. Certainly not someone in septic shock on so many drips."

A resident asked about a tracheostomy. "Won't that deliver an actual higher concentration of oxygen in the lung by decreasing the amount of dead space the ventilator has to push past?"

The Attending considered the thought. "It's possible it may help a little bit. A very little bit." He instructed the resident to call ENT and ask for a STAT consult for the surgical procedure. And he asked if anyone had seen the ID service that morning, but nobody had.

"Well page Doctor Auginello. Maybe the bug doctor can pull some kind of magic rabbit out of his microbiological hat."

<><><><><><>

Detective Williams was about to rap on the door to the office of the hospital chief of security when the door opened with a sudden jerk and a voice within barked, "I don't care how long it takes, Hopper, I want it done today. *Now!*"

Williams watched an anxious young guard flee the room and hurry down the corridor. Stepping into the office, he saw the familiar figure of Joe West, former Philadelphia police officer, now chief of hospital security, seated at a desk with a bank of video monitors mounted on the wall above the desk.

"Morning, West," said Williams. "Got a minute?"

Joe West eyed the detective warily. Without a word he gestured to an empty chair. Williams noted the gun strapped to West's belt and wondered if the man kept a second weapon strapped to his ankle beneath his pants. Wouldn't put it past him, West had always been a shifty cop.

"Looks like you've got pretty much the whole hospital wired for video surveillance," said Williams.

"Just about. We cover every section except the locker rooms and bathrooms. Some of the females are sensitive about an officer seeing them change their clothes."

"Have to respect their privacy" said Williams. Not relishing a sparring match with the cagey security chief, Williams decided to try and appeal to the man's ego.

"Reason I came by, Joe, I've got a puzzling case the ME dumped in my lap, and it's a sure bet you're the best man to get it unraveled. Think you can help me out?"

West turned his shark eyes on the Detective. "Depends on the issue. What's it about?"

"Louis Gordon. Fellow found hanging from a water pipe couple of days ago. You know the case."

"Sure I do. That was a suicide. I don't see what a homicide detective would be interested in it for."

"The ME's going to rule it a suspicious death. Hence, my coming to see you."

"Oh really? Suspicious. Looked like an open and shut case to me, the man was hanging from a rope, chair kicked over. I'd call it a classic case of self-induced death."

"You didn't see the autopsy. The ME says the evidence suggests foul play."

"What kind of evidence?"

"I didn't get all the details yet. He's still waiting for the toxicology report. You remember how slow the city labs are getting us results."

"Some things never change," said West.

"Indeed. Anyhow, the doc's suspicious, so I've got to ask, do you know of anyone who had a beef with the man? Did he owe any money? Sleep with some guy's wife, that sort of thing?"

West nodded his head slowly. "Y-e-a-h, he did have a beef with somebody. A big one. It seems the American born blacks and the ones from the Caribbean don't see eye to eye. They're always getting into fights. I'm surprised I haven't received a report of a gunshot victim."

"Some of them are packing?" said Williams.

"You better believe it. Last year one of the mopes shot up a dialysis holding tank. Reason we found out, the bullet leaked lead into the water and it showed up on the quality control tests."

"Think the shooter was aiming at Louie?"

"No way to know, but I wouldn't be surprised. They're all a bunch of animals down there."

Williams jotted a note on his smart phone. "Any particular names jump out?"

"One does. Dante Soleil. He worked with Louie in the dialysis unit. We never recovered a weapon, so we couldn't charge the little bastard."

Writing the name down, Williams asked if Louie had been involved in anything illegal. Drugs or theft of hospital property. West denied knowing anything about that, but he didn't think so.

"Louie was in trouble a lot, but usually it was just bullshit. Being away from his work area. Calling out sick on a weekend. That sort of thing."

"Okay, thanks." Williams handed West his business card. "Later today I want to review your security tapes from the day of the incident. Can you cue up the relevant video?"

"Of course. I'll have my tech man copy the video and have it waiting for you at, say, two o'clock?"

"That'll be great, I'll see you at two."

As soon as Detective Williams was gone, West got his IT officer, Stanley Winterbottom, on the phone and ordered him to cue up all the videos from the day of Louie's death and make a copy of them. "I want the videos set up for me in an hour." When the tech man complained it would take longer than that to even find the relevant footage from the multiple recordings from around the hospital, West told him to get it done or find another place to work.

TWENTY-FIVE

Lenny was sweeping up debris in front of the main entrance of the hospital and chatting with a worker from the laundry when he spied a beefy hospital security guard seated in a car on Germantown Ave with what looked like a video camera in his hand pointed at him. *Is that bastard taping me?* he wondered. Anger rising in his chest, Lenny told the laundry worker he had to take care of something and marched broom in hand down the hospital entrance toward the street. The guard in the car started the engine and pulled quickly out on the avenue, nearly hitting a car that was passing.

Lenny stood on the sidewalk watching the car drive away. He realized the man had been around a number of times when he was working. At the time he'd figured the guy had been assigned to his area in the hospital. So why was the bastard out on the street, *in a car,* watching him? And *why* was he apparently recording his work?

Realizing this must be a campaign by Joe West to find things to discipline him for, Lenny decided to ask Sandy the next time he saw him what was the hell was going on.

<><><><><><>

In response to an urgent consultation request, the ENT Attending and his retinue walked into the ICU. The Attending, a towering figure of a man with a broad chest and big, meaty hands, wasted no time, going directly to Fahim, who was updating his progress notes.

"Fahim. What's the big idea wasting my resident's time with this bullshit consult?"

His black eyes flashing, Fahim rose from his chair and asked the ENT doctor why did he think the request for a tracheostomy on

Mrs. Mudge was bullshit. A head taller than the ICU physician, the ENT doctor wagged a finger in Fahim's face.

"The god damned patient is on multiple pressors, she's got at least five organ systems failing, and she's older than Mother Teresa!"

"I agree, her condition is extremely critical. But she does not have a terminal disease. She doesn't have metastatic cancer or end-stage liver disease."

"The woman's circling the drain! How the hell is a tracheostomy going to turn around her septic shock?"

"If I can oxygenate her tissue a little better, she might turn around. She -"

"*You're* going all out because there's a lawsuit waiting in the wings. I know how she broke her hip. And I know all about the failure of the ortho team to recognize her medication history. Don't try to bring me in on this case, I don't need another subpoena, my malpractice insurance is already costing more than all my cars, *and* my mortgage!"

With that the ENT surgeon abruptly turned and stalked out of the ICU, taking his team with him, and leaving Dr. Fahim with no more options.

<><><><><><>

In the kitchen, Moose gave one of the cooks the union flyer attacking the decertification campaign. The cook, gray haired and stoop shouldered, looked at it and handed it back to Moose.

"What's the deal? You want to see the union out on its ass? You want to work with nobody watching your back?"

"It's not that, Moose," said the cook. "It's just, the hospital's gonna go outta business if we don't give 'em some concessions. Besides, they say without the union they can make up a lotta new job descriptions. They're gonna make me a chef first class. For more money."

"You believe that bullshit? All they want t' do is cut, cut, cut. They gonna make you chef and give you part-time work. With no benefits! You okay with that?"

"Long as I keep my job, I guess I'll have to be."

"Jesus. Doesn't it bother you they're asking you to cook with out of date ingredients?" Chicken past its use date?"

"Hey, long as we stew it all day, ain't nothin growin' in my food's gonna make nobody sick. They want me to put horse meat in the beef stew, I got no problem with that."

Moose left to go pick up the breakfast trays, shaking his head and bewildered at the stupidity of some people, pushing the big cart along the hall. Being sure he was not in the line of sight of one of the surveillance cameras, he grabbed a few flyers from inside the cart and dropped them in the employee lounge. He left some in the tiny pantry as well. And when he went to the nursing station to pick up more menus, he left flyers there as well.

An aide with a limp picked up a flyer and asked Moose what he thought was going to happen. "We lose the union, we could lose our workman's comp and unemployment," he said.

"Damn, I can't afford to be out of work with no pay," said the aide.

"Well you better spread the word, then, 'cause there's some folks blaming the union for the budget problems."

"I think the only budget problem is all the money going to the new boss," said the aide. "I heard they givin' him a million and a half to run the place. I sure could use some a' that money."

"Heh, heh. You and me both."

Moose pushed his cart to the service elevator, greeting co-workers along the way and asking them where they stood on the decertification campaign. Some were ambivalent, some for the union, some wanted to give the new administration a chance to 'fix' the money problems. He found hope in the ones who were solidly behind the union, but still worried at all the workers buying the company line.

<><><><><><>

Regis Devoe spent the start of his shift preparing the autopsy lab for a postmortem. But he had a raft of flyers tucked in his bag. When it was time to make the rounds picking up specimens for the pathology lab, he was ready to drop off flyers and engage the workers he met in conversation.

In the dialysis unit, Abrahm was not making much headway with the Jamaican techs, who were still skeptical that the dues they paid every month brought them any benefits. But the orderlies who brought patients into the unit were more receptive, so he quietly gave them copies of the flyer and asked them to think about what work would be like if they had nobody to stand with them when they faced discipline.

One older transporter who wore a waistband support agreed with Abrahm. After his surgery it was the union that got him light duty for three months until he was well enough to push a patient on a stretcher. He took several flyers and promised to leave them in the dispatch office for the other transporters.

Abrahm thought the tide was turning in their direction, although some departments, like security and the administrative clerical staff, were not convinced.

<><><><><><>

After leaving Joe West in the security office, Detective Williams decided he needed to talk to the people who cut Louie's body down and attempted to revive him. Although he didn't know where to go for that kind of information, he had one contact who knew everything that happened in the hospital. His contact sometimes held information back from him. But what he did give was always accurate and invaluable.

Riding the elevator to the seventh floor, he showed the

housekeeper on Seven South his police badge and asked where could he find Lenny Moss. Little Mary looked Williams up and down as if she was sizing him for a suit. Or, perhaps, a casket. "Lenny don't work on the ward no more. They done put him out on the grounds. Try outside the ER or the main entrance."

"Okay, thanks," said Williams.

As soon as the detective left, Little Mary went to the phone at the station and called Lenny to warn him. Lenny reassured her *he* wasn't in trouble with the law, it was bound to be about Louie's death.

"All right, I guess. Just so's they don't try and put nothin' on you," she said. "Them cops can't be trusted."

"I'll be careful, Mary, thank you."

Little Mary wasn't entirely reassured. The memory of the Move massacre, where the police set fire to a building where a radical back to the land group of black militants were barricaded in their house, was seared in her mind: especially the death of the children in the fire, the militants having been too frightened to leave the house, certain they would all be shot down by police snipers.

Well, Lenny was a good judge of character. If he trusted this one detective, maybe the man was all right. Mary would have to watch and see for herself if the man's word was good.

TWENTY-SIX

Mimi was at home doing the laundry and worrying about going back to work. She called Gary Tuttle, who used to work with her on Seven South before he moved to the ICU, and complained about the heavy patient load the nurses had to take on.

"It's no better in the unit," said Gary. "When I started we never had more than two patients, and if one of them was unstable we just took that patient. But now it's pretty much an everyday thing, one or two of us will have three patients. And if one of them is discharged, we get the admission."

Mimi said it was terrible what Croesus was doing. "I was shocked when I saw that bullshit petition to get rid of the service worker's union. They can't get away with that, can they?"

"Lenny says the threats to close the hospital are turning a lot of the members against the union."

"Gary, I'm scared for *my* job. The way they're tracking us with those damn GPS units, measuring our response time...It's not right! I didn't go into nursing to run track!" She told him how much her feet were hurting her by the end of her twelve hour shift. "I wish we had Lenny representing us. I wish *we* had a union."

"I don't think the nurses would ever go for it," said Gary. "Too many of them feel like they don't belong in a union."

"I know! It's so dumb! I heard a rumor they want to fire all the senior nurses and hire new grads, they're way cheaper."

"You're probably right," said Gary. There was a moment of silence. "You know, Mimi, organizing a nurse's union is not *impossible*. They did it in other hospitals."

"I know they did, Gary. But our nurses are so *scared*. I think they'd be too afraid of losing their job to ever come out for it."

After agreeing to talk about it the next time they were both on duty, Mimi said good-bye and began folding the laundry, dreading the idea of going back to work after the weekend and facing those damned dispatchers again.

<><><><><><>

Sandy came tootling down the driveway in his little electric cart and rolled up to Lenny, who was stuffing trash into a heavy-duty plastic bag.

"Yo, Lenny. How's the new assignment? You wearin' plenty of sun block out here on the street? You white fellas got to be careful, ya know. You don't want to come up with a case of skin cancer."

"Hi, Sandy," Lenny said, shaking hands with the old guard. "Yeah, it's great. Now I get to worry about skin cancer and getting hit by some drunk coming out the driveway."

Sandy chuckled, his hound dog jowls shaking. "Look on the bright side, man, you ain't got no supervisor lookin' over your shoulder every minute."

"I'm not so sure. No, I'm not sure at all." Lenny described the security guard who had been watching him. Sandy confirmed that it was Officer Jones.

"He's a lackey, all right," said Sandy. "Always sucking up to Joe West. That meat head'd do most anything West asked him to do."

"I think he's taping me."

"I ain't heard anything about that. But the other guards know I'm tight with you, so they'd be careful not to talk about it when I'm around." Sandy rubbed his shaved head and thought about it. "Yeah, I wouldn't put it past Joe West to try and catch you on tape doin' what you shouldn't be doin'. That's the kind of shit he'd do. 'Specially after that flyer you put out with the Nazi thing."

"That did have some strong language," said Lenny. "The union rep for our area Bob Feltcher chewed me out good for that one. Not that he didn't agree with it. But he has to worry about the union's liability."

"It sure made me sit up and take notice," said Sandy. "I wish I could've been a fly on the wall when the big bosses saw it. I bet they were blowin' steam out of their ears."

Lenny thanked Sandy and returned to his work. As he tied off the bag of trash , he felt the anger boiling up inside of him about the surreptitious videotaping. He was on the verge of leaving his post and marching to the Housekeeping office to confront his boss, Childress, when he saw a tall, familiar figure coming toward him.

"Jesus H. Christ," he muttered. "Just what I need."

Detective Williams held out a hand to Lenny, who removed his work glove and shook the officer's hand.

"Lenny Moss. Been a while since we've talked."

"It seems like only yesterday," said Lenny, leaning on the broom handle. "I guess you're here about Louie's murder."

Williams chuckled. "That's what I like about you, Lenny, you don't beat around the bush. And you're always in touch with what's going on inside." Williams looked down at the broom, dust pan and trash bag on the sidewalk, then back up at the hospital entrance. "How long've you been out here working the grounds."

"Since yesterday."

"Permanent?"

"As permanent as the job." Lenny explained that the administration was pushing a union decertification campaign, and that part of that campaign involved a security guard trailing him with a video camera.

"So this time Joe West is serious about getting rid of you."

"As serious as Louie hanging from a rope."

Williams asked Lenny what he knew about the death. Lenny confessed he knew nothing specific. "I've been so busy with the decert business, I haven't even *thought* about playing detective again."

"Well if that's true...If you really *are* going to stay out of my investigation, why don't you give me some background on the dead man?"

Considering the request, Lenny was surprised to discover that for once he was happy to let the police do the hard part, as long as Williams was in charge of the case. Lenny had learned through many an exchange with the detective that the man was more or less honest.

"Tell you what. You keep me up to date on what *you're* finding out, and I'll tell you everything I know that might bear on the case. Agreed?"

With the detective's agreement, Lenny told him about the shooting incidence in the dialysis unit: how one of the technicians - Lenny wouldn't say which one - had accidentally discharged a weapon, how the bullet had penetrated one of the holding tanks, and how the water had slowed the bullet so that it sank to the bottom of the tank.

"Joe West never found out who fired the gun?"

"He pretty much knew, but he had no proof, so there wasn't anything he could do about it.'

"That must have rattled his chain pretty good."

"West is always pissed about something." Lenny went on to tell Williams that Louie had been involved in low level drug sales in the hospital, and that he recently changed the beneficiary of his life insurance to his drug dealer."

"Dealer got a name?"

Lenny told him. "He drives for a car service, their dispatch is down the street from the hospital."

"Good cover for distribution," said Williams. "I'll check him out." The detective looked at his watch. "Listen, I need to talk to the doctors who discovered the body. I understand they cut him down. Something that had the Medical Examiner raising cane."

"Good luck getting anything out of those bozos. It was the big bosses making rounds, they were being inspected for accreditation. Doctor Slocum, the Chief Medical Officer, was there, plus Mother Burgess, the director of nursing."

Williams agreed, they probably wouldn't be ideal witnesses. But he had no other option. Thanking Lenny and turning to go, Lenny grabbed his arm and reminded him of his promise to keep Lenny up to date on the investigation.

"Oh, yeah. Well the ME found evidence of a severe asthma attack triggered by something he smoked that day."

"That would be the strychnine," said Lenny.

Williams did a double-take, smiled, shook his head. "Don't tell me you have a copy of the autopsy report."

"It's only a preliminary report, but, yeah, I've got a copy."

"You heard he had his asthma medicine on him when he died."

"Yeah, I knew that."

"Then I don't have anything more I can fill you in on. I asked West to cue up the video footage from the morning of the incident. He's supposed to have it ready for me after lunch."

"Wish I could watch it with you."

"So do I. Best I can do is tell you what I find." Williams thanked Lenny for his help, and returned to the hospital to seek out Dr. Slocum and Miss Burgess, anticipating a lot of bullshit and very little information.

<><><><><><>

Mr. Mudge sat beside Dr. Fahim listening to the ICU Attending list all the organs that had failed in his wife's body. Each additional organ failure increased the likelihood that she would not survive, until the number reached a frank certainty.

"I am sorry to have to tell you this, Mister Mudge. You are an educated man, you understand about these things. But your wife's prognosis is very, very poor. She is in my opinion in a terminal state. She will not recover."

Mr. Mudge slumped in his chair like a beaten man. He rubbed his hands together slowly, as if trying to warm them on a blustery day.

"I know, Samir. As soon as I heard she had fallen and broken her hip, I sensed it would be a downhill spiral. She hasn't taken care of herself for years, despite all my protestations."

"Wasn't she on meds for diabetes and for hypertension?"

"She filled the script, but she never took the pills. She said she didn't like the way they made her feel. *Feeling* good was more important to her than actually *being* good. I gave up arguing with her a long time ago.'"

"I am sad to hear you say that," said Fahim. "It is tragic when rational human beings rob themselves of the resources that will keep them healthy."

"We are only a little bit rational, when you get right down to it. I still smoke my pipe, after all."

"And I eat too much and have too much fat deposition in my belly. But to live without our vices..."

"Is to live chaste and without joy."

Fahim pulled a form from the chart, turned it around so that Mr. Mudge could read it, and placed it beneath the man's eyes. Mudge read the Do Not Resuscitate consent form without flinching.

When Fahim reached to his pocket to free a pen, Mudge waived him off. "I have my own," he said, withdrawing an old fashioned fountain pen; the kind you refilled from a bottle of ink. Pulling the cap from the pen, he looked up at Fahim. "There is no point prolonging the suffering." He signed with a flourish in a script that was barely legible.

Fahim was not sure if Mr. Mudge meant his wife's suffering or his own. Either way, the decision was right; further treatment was futile.

TWENTY-SEVEN

Joe West stood ramrod straight at the head of the conference table as Dr. Slocum held aloft a copy of the union flyer accusing the hospital of trying to break the union. "I want an end to this filth being disseminated in this facility, and I want the person responsible terminated and prosecuted to the fullest extent of the law!"

"It's awful. Just awful," said Miss Burgess. "It accuses *this* administration of secretly promoting the petition to remove the union. It's nothing but an attack upon this great facility and its leadership. I was nauseated when I read the document."

After more statements of revulsion and promises of unbridled support for the decertification petition, Housekeeping Director Norman Childress admitted he had personally searched Lenny Moss's locker and the supply closet on Seven-South where Lenny used to work, but found no copies of the flyer there.

Martin Freely, Director of Human Resources, called for reason and patience. "I agree, this is almost certainly the work of Mister Moss and his associates. But let me remind you, a man is still considered innocent until proven guilty, and we have no objective proof that he was the direct author of it."

"We don't need proof of his guilt in order to terminate him," said West. "Look at this document, it will remove any doubts you may have." West handed out a copy of his investigation into Lenny's movements. "You will see the times that Mister Lenny Moss was away from his assigned post without approval from his supervisor. Also note the photographs of him at those unauthorized locations, which were culled from video coverage I have a total of six instances of him being away from his work area without authorization."

"That's all well and good," said Slocum. "But I want to see

pictures of him handing out those dirty flyers. They denigrate the hospital and they poison employee morale. I want Moss's head on a platter for the scurrilous things on it!"

West stood patiently, observing the physician with cold eyes. "Lenny Moss is no fool, doctor. He hasn't given out the flyers himself, he has his flunkies do it for him."

"Can't you catch some of them in the act and turn them against him?" asked Burgess.

"So far they have been cagey. I don't have anything on videotape. But I will. Soon."

"Not good enough!" cried Slocum. "Dr. Reichart was frothing at the mouth this morning, telling me he wants the union propaganda killed. Stopped. Dead and buried."

Mr. Freely coughed quietly, turning everyone else's gaze in his direction.

"I beg your pardon," he said. "Does everyone really believe that getting rid of one union organizer will derail the opposition to the decertification drive?" Freely looked from face to face.

"It will throw the fear of god into the rest of them!" said Childress. "My housekeepers depend on Moss to give them courage. Without him, they'll fall to pieces."

"Cut off the head of the snake," said Slocum. "It's the most effective approach."

Freely wiped his brow with a lavender handkerchief. "But even if terminating the man will blunt the opposition, you're going about it in the worst possible way. Singling out one person and following him with surreptitious videotaping...It's wrong. It's monstrous."

"Don't be ridiculous," said West. "Surveillance is a proven investigative tool. Police have won court cases time and time again using hidden cameras and wiretaps."

Freely's mouth dropped open. "I hope you aren't secretly taping *his* phone calls."

"Of course not. What do you think we are, the Gestapo?" West waved a hand in front of his face. "Everything we do is strictly legal. Moss will have no grounds for appealing his termination, you can depend on it."

Slocum turned to Mr. Freely. "Martin, I want you to call Moss to Human Resources and give him his notice of termination. I want it done today."

Freely dabbed his forehead again. His stomach was turning summersaults and his vision was becoming blurry. He had handled termination meetings countless times in his career as director of Human Resources. Many clearly deserved it. Employees who worked drunk or high were a danger to the patients. One supply clerk had piled his cart so high he couldn't see over the top and then careened down the hall with his iPod blaring music in his ears. He knocked over an elderly woman who was visiting a relative and broke her hip.

A safe hospital environment required the hospital staff to maintain some minimal standard of sobriety and mental alertness. Freely knew that Lenny Moss was no threat to the patients. He was only a threat to the machinations and ruthless tactics of Croesus and the new administration.

"I, I'm sorry, I cannot do it," said Freely. Slocum's face showed a stunned look.

"What do you mean, you can't do it?" said the physician. "I'm giving you an order, there's nothing to discuss. You *must* fire that pesky janitor."

Freely closed the notebook he had brought for taking notes, rose, and faced his boss. "Doctor Slocum, I regret that there are some actions that even I cannot bring myself to take. I hope that you will reconsider your decision." He rose from his chair and quietly left the conference room.

West growled, "I'll do it. Get me the paper work."

"No, let me!" said Childress, Lenny's supervisor.

Childress, you take care of it," said Slocum. "West, you go with him. Hand Moss his walking papers and escort him off the grounds."

As West rose and stepped to the door, Childress stood up and followed him out of the room without a word. The two men understood each other perfectly. They shared a pitiless, take-no-prisoners approach to life and were made from the same cloth: sharkskin. West led Slocum out the door, happy to do the bidding of a merciless leader.

Slocum slumped in his chair while Burgess patted his hand, assuring him he was doing the only thing that made sense, for the good of the hospital. He felt his migraine expand into a consuming super nova of pain. He was about to return to his office for a dose of pain medicine, and a drink, when his beeper went off. The call had come from his secretary, and it had a 911suffix attached to it.

Calling the number, he listened to his secretary, then hung up. Miss Burgess asked what was it about.

"Just what I need to really screw up my day. There's a goddamned Philadelphia police detective waiting to see me in my office."

Burgess walked to her boss and put an arm around his shoulder. "It's probably about that annoying little man who hung himself. I'm sure it's just the police's routine follow-up. They need to write a report, is all."

Slocum shook his head. "Christ. Why couldn't he kill himself at home like a normal person?"

<><><><><><>

Dr. Slocum's shoulders sagged when he saw the tall, imposing figure of police detective Williams standing in the outer office. Ushering the officer in, Slocum sank into his deep leather chair, picked up a pen and tapped the desk top, waiting.

Williams wasted no time getting to the point. He wanted to know why they had interfered with the crime scene and cut down the body. Slocum threw up his hands. "Are you kidding me? Leave a man hanging by his neck when there might be a chance to resuscitate him? I can't do that, I have a moral *and* a legal obligation to do anything I can to preserve a life!"

Williams put on a sympathetic face. "I can understand your commitment to prudent medical practice, doctor. But didn't you determine right off the bat that the body was cold? The ME estimated the time of death to be at least ten hours before you discovered him."

"I wasn't thinking about that. There were inspectors with us, everyone was tense. I reacted, that's all. Nobody can blame me for trying."

Williams asked if Slocum knew the deceased.

"Never saw him before."

"You wouldn't recognize his name, then?"

"No. I understand he was a lowly technician who serviced the dialysis machines. I would have no reason to know him."

Williams asked about the friction between the American born and the Caribbean born black workers in the hospital. Slocum swore that the hospital had an affirmative action program and an anti-discrimination program that weeded out prejudice on every level.

Seeing he would get nothing more useful from the physician, Williams left to go to the dialysis unit where Louie had worked.

TWENTY-EIGHT

Lenny was not surprised when he was called to the Housekeeping office for a meeting with Childress. With the flyers going around and the clandestine video taping of him, he was certain the boss was gunning for him.

Entering his boss's office, Lenny smelled the air freshener and the underlying hint of whiskey. Joe West was standing in front of the boss's desk, his silver handcuffs dangling from his belt just waiting to be used.

"Don't bother to sit down, Moss, you won't be here long enough," said Childress.

"I prefer to stand, thanks." Seeing a copy of the flyer attacking the decertification drive on Childress's desk, Lenny had a good idea what was coming.

"You're fired, Moss. Terminated as of today. Mister West will escort you to your locker where you can empty out anything that doesn't belong to the hospital, and then he'll show you the door."

"What's the charge?"

Childress picked up the flyer and held it at arm's length as though it was contaminated with some dreadful germ. "We know you're behind the scurrilous attacks on the hospital. It has your teeth marks all over it. You can't bite the hand that feeds you and not expect to be bit back."

"Oh, yes, I saw one of those highly informative leaflets somewhere or other. Funny, though, I didn't see my name on it."

"Don't be cute, we know you wrote it."

"I see. You know that because you identified the lower case 'i' that's missing the dot in my old Royal typewriter with the worn out ribbon? Is that how you nabbed me?"

Childress reached out and snatched the identification badge from Lenny's shirt. "Always the wise guy, aren't you, Moss? Always the smart answer. Didn't your father ever tell you, you keep mouthing off, somebody's gonna knock that smile off your face?"

"Actually, my dad taught me to join the fight for justice wherever it's needed."

"You know the drill. You will empty your locker, *under supervision,* and march your sorry ass out of this facility."

West withdrew a form from a folder and held it out for Lenny. "This is your notice of termination. Sign it."

"No, thanks. Without any evidence against me, I'll win my appeal at the third step meeting."

"Read the fine print, Moss. You've been seen away from your assigned post without permission on six occasions in two days. You know the contract. You can't go off duty without permission from your supervisor."

"Yeah, I saw your security man playing plainclothes detective. I know you've been taping me. That's another strike against you."

"I don't think so," said Childress. "I think this time we've got you by the balls, and your shit ass union can't do a thing about it."

West escorted Lenny out of Childress's office and accompanied him to the locker room, where he watched as Lenny emptied the contents of his locker into a large trash bag. West inspected every item, from the dog-eared copy of the contract, folders with records of grievances Lenny had filed, a spare set of shoes and sox, and a couple of paperback books.

Tying off the bag, Lenny hoisted it over his shoulder like a sailor and was about to head out when Abrahm came in.

"Lenn'ye, what is this? What is happening?"

"They're firing me, Abrahm."

"Oh, this is turrible. Turrible! What dogs! What fascists!"

"Yeah, well, it won't last, I'll file an appeal and be back on the job within a week."

"I hope so Len'nye. I will tell everyone what they have done. Everyone!"

Thanking his friend, Lenny made his way to the loading platform accompanied by Officer Jone. On the platform a worker with heavy, puncture-proof gloves was picking up the medical waste to take to a medical grade incinerator. Lenny felt like he could be heading for the same destination.

As soon as he was out on Germantown Ave, Lenny called Moose to tell him what had happened and asked him to bring some workers to Lenny's house that evening. His friend promised to be there, with Regis and Little Mary and a bottle of Jack Daniels.

<><><><><><>

Detective Williams passed Abrahm, who was cleaning a reclining chair in the dialysis treatment room, and stepped into the work room, where he found Dante cleaning a machine and replacing the internal, disposable parts. While the young man worked, ignoring Williams, the detective looked over the big holding tanks. He found the one with the patch where a bullet from a gun Dante had fired the year before had made a hole and ran his finger over the patch.

Satisfied, Williams asked the young man to take a few minutes to answer some questions. In private. Dante shrugged, put down his tools, and accompanied the police officer to the isolation room, which was empty.

"I won't beat around the bush. I hear you and Louis Gordon didn't get along. He pissed you off big time telling security that you were the guy who fired off a weapon at work. That so?"

Dante shrugged again and ran the back of his hand over his mouth, as if he'd just tasted something unpleasant.

"Wasn't no big thing. I was pissed off sure, but I let it go. You can't hold on to your anger, mon, it eats you up inside. You ever hear that?"

Williams ignored the rhetorical question. "I've been told you're not the kind of man who forgets things."

"Somebody mixin' me up with somebody else. I'm for peace

and love, like Marley sings about. We got to bring peace to the earth with music."

Sizing up the suspect, Williams told him he could cut the BS and give some straight answers or come down to the precinct and spend the night in a cell. When Dante said he heard the food was getting better in jail, it wasn't just two pieces of dry white bread with a big hunk of cheese in the middle, Williams said he was an inch away from charging Date with Louie's murder.

"You have an alibi for the night he was killed? 'Cause the District Attorney likes you for this crime. He likes you real good. So unless you can come up with a solid explanation of where you were , it's time for handcuffs and a ride in the back of the car."

"I was home watching the game. I got a big flat screen, can see the seams on the ball nice and clear."

"Anybody with you?"

"Just me by my lonesome."

"Anybody call you?"

"No calls, I turn my phone off when the game is on. Don't want to be distracted."

Williams debated hauling Dante down to the precinct for more questioning. But he had to admit, there was no evidence of any kind to justify it. Motive, he had. But so far nobody had come forward claiming to have seen him in the hospital that night. And there was no forensic evidence yet suggesting that Dante was anywhere near the room where Louie died.

After the detective exited the dialysis unit, Abrahm watched Dante come out of the room and head for the men's bathroom. He watched with great sympathy. And with fear the police would once again arrest the wrong man for the crime.

Abrahm found a secluded spot and dialed Lenny, who was on his speed dial. Number one.

<><><><><><>

As soon as Moose heard from Lenny about the termination, he walked through the hospital letting his co-workers know about it. Abrahm, Regis, Little Mary and others joined in spreading the news, which quickly reached every department. The workers were shocked, angry, depressed and all of the above. Several asked what the union was doing about it. Moose was certain the union would appeal. But since he didn't know what evidence they had against his friend, he couldn't assure everyone that Lenny would win his case.

But then he remembered what Lenny had been telling him for years: that a termination is rarely overturned just on the merits of the legal case. It depended more on the political muscle of the union; on how much support the individual had among the rank and file; and on how many workers the union could bring to the hearing in a show of support.

Moose recalled with a smile the time they all wanted to go to the funeral of a beloved worker, but the service was being held during the week in the middle of the day. When Childress rejected Lenny's request to give the workers an extra hour for lunch to attend the service, he and Moose and others organized a march on the president's office. The power of that group had been so great, the president readily granted Lenny's request, which resulted in the workers not only attending the service, but staying for food and plenty of drinks, and returning just in time to punch out.

Reaching Seven South, Moose found Little Mary, who had already heard the news and spread it to everyone on the floor.

"What we gonna do?" she cried. We got t' get him back! We need Lenny!"

Moose told her they were meeting at Lenny's house that evening to plan the fight to get him back on the job. That reassured Mary, who promised to be there.

"All the times he had my back, you know I'll be there for Lenny. You *know* I will."

Moose continued his rounds, encouraged that workers like Little

Mary were ready to go to the wall for his friend. The bell had rung, the bosses had sucker punched Lenny and put him on the mat, but the crowd was calling for paybacks. And justice.

TWENTY-NINE

The union organizing committee met at Lenny's house, where they agreed they had to go on the offensive. It began with Moose, Regis and Abrahm describing the responses they were getting on the flyer attacking the decertification drive. Little Mary said when she heard anybody expressing a lack of support for the union, she cursed them out and threatened to knock them silly if they didn't get on the bus.

"Now that Lenny's out, we got t' carry on 'til he's back," she said. "'Cause he comin' back, ain't no two ways around it, Lenny's comin' back!"

Lenny reiterated his concern that it would help them if they could pin Croesus to the decertification campaign. They knew in their guts who was behind it, but they needed hard evidence if they were going to file and win an unfair labor practice complaint with the Labor Relations Board.

Patience, setting down a plate of homemade oatmeal cookies, said, "I bet there are people who know stuff. They're just too scared to talk to me or Moose or Lenny. I think we have to convince them to come forward and tell us who in the administration is fronting this dirty campaign."

"I agree," said Regis. "But I don't know how we're gonna convince them, they'll be out of a job if they talk."

"Not if they make it anonymous," said Lenny. "I think we should put out the word that people who know something about the decert campaign can send me an anonymous letter. Give out my mailing address."

Lenny was about to continue when the door bell rang. Malcolm, who had been sitting at the top of the stairs listening, ran down, yelling "I got it!"

The child let in Mimi, Gary Tuttle and Crystal. Lenny rose to welcome the three nurses while Patience and Birdie brought in extra chairs for them.

"Well, this is a surprise," said Lenny once the newcomers were seated and offered drinks. "Are you here to help fight the decert campaign?"

"Um, yes, and no," said Mimi, glancing at Crystal. Crystal told him that, while they were behind his union one hundred percent, they were taking so much heat, working in such difficult, unsafe conditions, they believed they needed a union, too.

Lenny looked at Gary, whom he knew well, the two having worked together on several investigations. With the look on his face of a minister who just converted a bunch of nonbelievers, Gary said, "We've been talking. We think this could be the best time for the nurses to organize a union of our own. Croesus is imposing such punitive working conditions on us, we're all fed up. Everybody's angry, they just don't know how to get something started."

"This is good, Tuttle. This is really good. We don't just fight to keep what we have, we go on the offensive."

"I knew you'd like the idea," said Mimi. "What nurse's union do you think we should apply to?"

"Well," said Lenny. "There are several unions for nurses. California has a highly respected organization. But I think we'd be in the best position to fight those bastards if you joined our union."

"I didn't know your union accepted RNs," said Mimi.

"Several hospitals have nurses in a separate division of our union. They're in different bargaining units, but we try to schedule our contracts to expire at the same time. And even when they don't, being in the same union, we each honor the other's picket line, if it comes to that."

"Going on strike - that's really dangerous," said Crystal. "I mean for the patients as much as for us. There are laws about nurses abandoning their patients that can lose us our license."

"It wouldn't be like that. If it did come down to a strike, and given how cold-blooded and anti-union Croesus is, we need to all be prepared for a strike, if we *did* call for a strike, it wouldn't be a walkout. We'd give the hospital notice so they could arrange to discharge patients beforehand."

"Or bring in a bunch a' scabs," said Moose. "You know they got all these temporary agencies with nurses who are willing to cross a picket line. They even fly them in from other states."

"I hear they bring in nurses from other countries," said Mary. "Chinese nurses!"

Crystal confirmed that in some places hospitals recruited nurses from overseas, but with the current cuts in hospital beds and hospital closings, that was becoming less common.

Mimi asked what did they need to do to bring in the union. Lenny said the union had already scheduled an emergency meeting for Saturday at noon. He invited the three of them to attend.

"I'll ask the regional director to invite the organizer from the nursing division to attend. We can present your proposal at the same time we discuss what to do about stopping the decertification."

Amid more discussion of the issues and plans for organizing, bottles of wine and a bottle of Jack Daniels were passed around, with everyone partaking. Patience brought out a tray with toast covered with cheese and bacon and set it down on the coffee table. "Bacon and cheese is Malcolm's favorite," she said. "And Lenny's." She watched with satisfaction as everyone grabbed the snacks and wolfed them down.

<><><><><><>

After the last visitors had gone and the children were put to bed, Patience told Lenny that in the morning they should look over their budget and see where they stood. She usually balanced the checkbook and paid the bills, Lenny did the food shopping and the laundry.

Lenny kissed her gently on the cheek. "You don't have to worry, Moose got me a job."

"What? *Already*? What is it?"

"Cleaning office rooms in Center City for a temp agency. His cousin works there."

"That Moose and his cousins."

"It's night work, I can start Saturday night. I work nine at night to five in the morning."

"Five in the morning."

"Yeah."

"Well at least it's a job." Patience sat on the bed and began rubbing lotion into her legs.

"You okay with my being out all night working?" said Lenny. "I can look for something else if you're not comfortable with it."

"No, no, you have to take it, jobs aren't easy to find out there. Especially for a man who's been fired."

Lenny took a squeeze of the lotion and rubbed it into the sole of her foot.

"Lenny."

"Huh?"

"Remember the time your dad got sick and you dropped out of college to help your mom pay the bills?"

"Yeah..."

"I wish I'd known your dad, he sounds like a great guy."

"He was. I wouldn't be who I am if it wasn't for him."

She glanced at a picture of Lenny's mom and dad on the dresser across the room. "Well, don't you think he would have wanted you to finish your degree?"

"I don't know. I suppose so. Why?" He rubbed some lotion into her other foot.

"Don't misunderstand me, I think you'll get your job back. I have faith you will."

"O-kay."

"But you can't go on being a steward and getting beat up and putting your life in danger forever. What about finishing your degree in history and teaching? Like you wanted to do when you were young?"

"I'm not that knowledgable about history. People who teach it are steeped in that stuff. I'm just an amateur."

Amateur? You read history all the time, the house is loaded with the books you read."

"Okay, I dabble in it. But that's not - "

"You do a whole lot more than dabble Lenny. You know a lot."

"I still don't know all that much about history. It's a huge field."

"But you know a lot about *labor history.*"

"I've read a bit."

"You know all about how unions were formed. And how those super rich guys - what do you call them?"

"The robber barons?"

"Yes! The robber barons. You know how they tried to kill the unions when they were being born. That's very relevant today! You've said so yourself.'

"Yes, it's relevant."

"So you could teach labor history. To unions and in colleges. Maybe high school."

"I'd have to get a masters degree at least. That'd take years and years."

"You have years and years ahead of you." She stopped abruptly, recalling the age of Lenny's father when he died unexpectedly of a stroke.

"Lenny, don't you think you're going to live to be an old man?"

Lenny sat quietly for a moment. Finally he said, "To be honest, I always figured I'd go kind of early, the way my old man did."

"Well I"m not going to let that happen. You're going to grow old and grey along with me, and enjoy our grandchildren. And our retirement. So you might as well start taking those college classes you need, 'cause it's going to be a long ride to the end."

Lenny kissed his wife on the cheek and promised to give

it some thought after he got through with the fight against the decertification campaign.

Turning the light out, Patience lay awake for a long time. She knew that there would *always* be another campaign. Always another struggle. Probably more crimes to investigate, too. If she was going to convince Lenny to earn his degree and move out of hospital work and into teaching, it was going to be a long, hard campaign. Just like the campaign to keep the union.

"There's just one thing that worries me."

"Oh, what's that?"

"I know you're going to want to work like crazy all day long on the union campaign and on getting your job back. But you *have* to get enough sleep."

Lenny said it wouldn't be a problem.

"It's really important, Lenny, I'm not playing with you. You *must* allow time to sleep or you'll put yourself back in the hospital."

Lenny promised to be good, kissed her, and went to brush his teeth, wondering how any man ever survived without a wife like his Patience.

THIRTY

On Saturday morning, while Patience and Takia ate a healthy cereal with low fat milk and fresh berries, Lenny cooked French toast in a pool of butter for himself and Malcolm. He told Patience he was going to take the money they'd raised over to Matilda, Louie's widow, after breakfast.

"Aren't you going jogging with Moose this morning?"

"I called and canceled, I've got too much to do. Besides, it looks like rain."

"People jog in the *rain,*" said Patience. "I think a run would do you good."

"Maybe tomorrow. I've got to prepare for the a union meeting this afternoon. Did you get a baby-sitter."

Malcolm protested that he was old enough he didn't need a baby-sitter, a claim Takia, two years older, seconded, but Patience waved them off.

Settling a pair of toast on Malcolm's plate, Lenny slathered it with a mixture of maple syrup, brown sugar and butter, his own culinary invention.

"Mmm-mm," said Malcolm, anxious for that first exquisite bite of crisp toast dripping sweet syrup. Patience rolled her eyes and went back to reading the morning paper.

Malcolm looked worried, he wasn't wolfing down his favorite breakfast like usual. Lenny asked him what was up.

"Nothin'," said Malcolm, stirring a piece of toast in the pool of syrup.

"Come on. I know *something's* on your mind."

"Well..." The boy poked a finger in the syrup and licked it. "Now that you don't have a job, are we gonna have to move out the house?

"But I'm not out of a job."

"You *ain't*?" Malcolm saw his mother glaring at his use of the contraction and looked away from her. "But I thought they done fired you."

"They did. But they're not going to get away with it. The union is going to fight to get me my job back. And in the meantime, Moose got me a job cleaning offices down in Center City. In fact, I start tonight."

"You won't be here at *night*?"

"No, Malcolm, I won't. So I was hoping you would kind of keep an eye on the place, you being the only man at home while I'm gone. Will you do that for me?"

"Sure!" Malcolm stabbed three pieces of toast, dipped them in the thick syrup and filled his mouth until his cheeks puffed out. He chewed happily, imagining what it will be like to be the man in charge all night long.

<><><><><><>

Seeing the button for the door bell was pulled out and not functioning, Lenny knocked on the door of the little house in North Philly and waited. After a moment a woman's voice called, "Who there?"

"It's me, Lenny. From the hospital. Remember?"

The door opened, revealing a heavy-set, woman with thick makeup on her brown face and wearing a red wig.

"Oh, hi, Lenny. Sure, I remember you, you always organized the Christmas parties at the union hall. Sure, come on in."

Matilda stepped away from the door and let him in. The small living room was packed with dark wooden furniture, mirrors on the wall and a plump red sofa with a clear plastic covering.

"Sit yourself down there on the sofa, take a load off a' your feet," she said. "So nice of you to visit me like this. So *nice*."

"How's it going, Matilda? Is your family here? Are they giving you support?"

"Yeah, well, you know family," she said, settling into the other side of the sofa. "Everybody gives with one hand and takes with the other."

Lenny nodded, having been through too many funerals of his coworkers.

"How are the plans for the funeral coming? Have you got a date yet? A lot of people want to come to the ceremony."

"That's just it, Lenny, the city won't tell me when they're gonna give Louie up. He's still in the city morgue!"

"I know. It's part of the police investigation. They'll turn him over to the funeral home when they finish all the tests."

Matilda lit a cigarette and offered Lenny one, which he declined.

"Listen, I have something for you," he said, taking a thick manila envelope out of his backpack. "We got some donations from the workers. It's not all that much, but, still, every little bit helps." He handed her the envelope. Matilda peeked inside, saw the thick wad of bills. Her eyes filled with tears.

"This so nice, Lenny. This is so good. You have a lot of good Christian souls working in that place. I know Louie had his problems with the Jamaicans in his department. But I always knew there was others there that respected him."

"He had a lot of friends, Matilda. A whole lot of people came forward and wanted to donate."

She put the envelope in a drawer and settled back down. They sat in silence for a few moments. Finally, Lenny asked if she had any idea that Louie was in enough trouble to lead someone to want to take his life.

Matilda dabbed at her puffy eyes. "He was scared, Lenny. Louie was real scared."

"Of his dealer, you mean?"

"Yeah, of Roland Weekes, sure, that goes with the territory. But he was even more scared of somebody else."

"Who?"

"I don't know his name, but he worked in the security office.

That much I know."

"Was it Joe West?"

"Louie never said his name.."

"What was he scared about?"

"A day before he died, Louie went to pick up some weed from a guard in the security office. You know he smoked a little and he sold a little. But never anything big! And never any of them hard drugs like crack cocaine and such. Louie was strictly small time weed."

"That's pretty much what I've been hearing."

"Uh-huh. So anyway, when Louie went to pick up the weed, the guard was on the phone talking to somebody and he had some papers on the desk, and Louie saw the papers had something to do with getting rid of the union."

"That would be the decertification program."

"I guess so. The guard saw Louie looking at the papers, and he told him he was a dead man if he breathed a word about it to anyone. He said Joe West wouldn't just have him fired and arrested, he'd cut him up in pieces and feed them to the fishes out in the Delaware Bay. And Louie knew Joe West didn't play, that man is serious trouble."

"So Louie was afraid of West, not his dealer."

Matilda dabbed her eye again. "You know how much he loved you, Lenny. The way you always came through for him and you never judged him. Never bad mouthed him or nothin'. He wanted to tell you about it, but he couldn't, they would've killed him. So he and me decided we was gettin' out. For good."

"You were going to leave town?"

"Yup. You know that little piece a' property I inherited down North Carolina?"

"Of course. Louie was always talking about how he was going to move down there with you after he retired and build it up."

"Well he put a deposit down on a trailer. We were gonna have it towed to the site and move on down there. And then Louie was gonna build on it. You know, add other rooms an' all. And we were gonna make a new start."

She put a hand on Lenny's chest and touched her forehead to his shoulder. "He was gonna tell you everything soon as we got outta Dodge. He called me the night he was killed. Said he was putting in his papers and quitting. That was the last I heard from him. That he was putting in his papers and saying good-bye James Madison."

"West must have heard about his plan to quit and gotten rid of him."

"Can you prove it, Lenny? Can you bring that evil man down once and for all?"

"I don't know, Matilda. But I'm going to give it my best shot." He got up from the sofa. "I have to go, I have a lot of things to do, we're having a union meeting later today and I need to prepare for it."

"I understand." She walked him to the door, put her arms around him and hugged him tightly. He thought he might be there for hours. Finally she released him, looked up into his eyes and said, "You'll come to the funeral, won't you? You'll speak at the service?"

"Of course. Let me know the where and when, I'll bring as many coworkers as I can."

Leaving the house, Lenny felt he had something to go on: Louie had seen something that linked Joe West to the anti-union campaign. If he could get something solid - something tangible - they could use it to break the decertification petition and keep the union in place.

But how to find it?

And who was the guard that Louie had seen with the incriminating material?

THIRTY-ONE

Looking out at a sea of hospital workers, Lenny marveled, as he had many times before, how lucky he was to organize with a union that had such diversity and that stood for something. A union that wasn't just after the dues payment and a fat salary for the president and his henchmen.

Bob Feltcher, the area director, stepped to the podium to call the meeting to order. He wasn't a big man. At five feet eight inches, Feltcher wouldn't strike fear into an angry drunk in a bar or a racist at a civil rights demonstration calling him the N word and a whole lot worse. But the veteran organizer had the heart of a lion, the soul of a poet, and the voice of a jazz singer.

As Feltcher held up his hands, a hush fell over the crowd. "Anybody here support the, what is it, the Committee To Save James Madison?"

"*NO!*" cried the membership.

"That's good. Because all any of us here want to do is to *save* your hospital, and kicking out our union will do exactly the opposite. It will destroy it. Health and safety? Out the window! Respect for seniority? Gone fishing! Benefits and vacation accrual? Sayonara! But you know what you *will* get if they destroy this union? Increased work loads! Mandatory overtime! Forced weekend duty! Part time benefits while working sixty hours a week! *That's what you'll get if that bullshit committee wins their vote to decertify this great union!*"

The rank and file stood up and cheered, cried, stomped their feet and clapped their hands. They were fired up and ready to fight.

"This decert campaign is an attack on the workers, it's an attack on the patients, and it's an attack on the democratic principles of union representation of working men and women. We have to send Croesus a message. We don't need to just vote down their campaign, we need to convince our brothers and sisters who have mistakenly signed the petition to take their names *back*!"

More cheers and hollers erupted throughout the hall.

Lenny stood up and asked to be recognized. "Mister Feltcher, I agree that we need to beat back their decertification campaign. And I can think of no better way to do that than to launch an organizing drive for the registered nurses at James Madison. In fact, we have with us in the hall three nurses from the hospital who want to be a part of that organizing drive."

Mimi, Gary and Crystal stood up, to cheers, whistles and hoots from the crowd.

Feltcher said that organizing the nurses was an important principle the union stood behind, but he wasn't sure this was the best time to do it. He cautioned that defeating the decertification drive was the issue they needed to deal with at the moment, after which they could move on the nurses' recruitment. But Lenny wouldn't have any of it.

"With all respect, I think we can't afford to play defense, that's a losing strategy," said Lenny. "The best defense is a good offense. Croesus only respects strength. We take the offense and invite the nurses to join us or they'll roll over us."

One worker worried that trying to organize the nurses would take away from their own union. "Some of them nurses look down on me," she said. "They think they better. What makes you think they'll support *us* if *we* go out on strike?"

Mimi raised her hand and was recognized by the chair. "I hear what you're saying. And I won't deny, some of us nurses have a superiority complex. But that's changing! And it's changing fast. Nurses are learning we're no better than any other employee in the hospital. We're all just cogs in a wheel to Croesus. The more they take away our autonomy and our dignity, the more we'll see we all have a common enemy and a common purpose."

Crystal added that she wished she had been in a union for ages but never thought her fellow nurses would support her. Now the whole workplace was changing, and in a bad way. In a way that undermines the nurse's authority.

Gary Tuttle rose and took his turn at the microphone. "With all due respect, sir, I believe that now is the best possible time to begin giving out union cards to the nurses. They are angry. They are scared. They are suffering. They need the support of their coworkers, and the best way in my judgment to win that support is for all of us to pull together. The nurses should sign a petition calling the decertification drive exactly what it is, a sham, a phony, a make-believe committee that's really led by Mother Burgess and Doctor Slocum. That will help us learn to all work together. We support you, and you support us."

Moose rose to his feet, lifted his fist in the air and declared, "I say we put it to the membership and vote on it. Do we want to organize the nurses into our union? Or do we want to see them driven into the dirt, with nobody to defend them?"

More cheers and applause filled the union hall. Bob Feltcher leaned over and spoke to the union treasurer, who had been on the phone with the union president. After a brief discussion, the director agreed to call a vote.

"All those who support launching a union organizing drive among the registered nurses at James Madison Medical Center, so signify by saying 'aye'."

"AYE!" The hall was rocked with a thunderous cry, followed by applause, whistles, slaps on the back and laughter.

"What about Lenny?" cried Little Mary. "I wanna know what you gonna do about gettin' him his job back. That's gotta be job one."

Feltcher nodded his head. "We have a grievance filed that we're prepared to take to arbitration if we lose at Step Three. What they did to our union steward was outrageous. They stalked him. They spied on him. They recorded him without his permission using hidden video cameras. I have no doubt we will win and Lenny will be reinstated with full back pay."

"We got to remind people, what they did to Lenny they could do to any one of us," said Regis.

"Good point," said Fetcher. "It's a matter of human dignity."

The members rose to their feet and shouted, *"DIGNITY!"* Then they applauded and whooped and hollered: the campaign to defeat decertification and organize the nurses was taking off.

<><><><><><>

After the meeting broke up Rose, the nursing division organizer told Mimi, Gary and Crystal she wanted to meet with them to learn more about their issues. They agreed to meet at Lenny's house Sunday morning.

Bob Feltcher took Lenny aside and told him the union had to send a letter of apology for the flyer the workers had given out in the hospital. "That Third Reich comment, it was over the top, Lenny. Not that I disagree with it, the man's a fascist, no question about it. But you've got to be careful how you word things if you have the union name on the flyer."

"Yeah, we debated keeping that in," said Lenny. "I just thought it would be good for once to say it like it is. Kind of the way you did in that book of yours about unions raiding other members."

Feltcher chuckled. "I took some serious heat from our president on that, even though the book was not about *our* union, it was more the decline of union membership overall because of the issues I discussed."

The area rep suggested that Lenny take a try at writing something more substantial than a flyer or the occasional letter in the union newspaper. Lenny thanked him and promised to consider it when the current struggle was settled, one way or the other.

Moose and Regis wanted to go out for a drink after the meeting, but Patience drove them off, saying, "Lenny's got to get some sleep, he's going to work tonight! What's wrong with you two, you want him to get sick?"

Lenny saw there was no point arguing with his wife. Besides, he *was* tired. A long afternoon nap was just what he needed. He walked to his car, Patience beside him, thinking about that soft, comfortable bed waiting for him at home and wishing he could sleep all the way through 'til morning.

THIRTY-TWO

Patience and Malcolm laid out plates, cups and silverware on the dining room table in anticipation of the morning's guests. The smell of bacon sizzling on a skillet mixed and the scent of freshly brewed coffee filled the room with heady aromas. As Patience counted out the chairs to make sure they had enough for the meeting, Lenny came in the front door balancing a bag of bagels in one hand and a bag of groceries in the other.

"I got brown eggs, think that's okay?" he called, heading for the kitchen. "And goat cheese and green onions for the omelet."

"Brown or white, the *egg* is the same," said Patience, following him. She stood in the doorway watching him set out the groceries. "Lenny, are you *sure* you're up for a meeting with the nurses, you just worked a whole night shift."

"I feel great!" Seeing the skeptical look on her face, he said he really wasn't tired, he was too excited about the new organizing drive to sleep, and he promised to take a long nap as soon as the meeting was over.

Putting the bagels in a wicker basket, he heard the doorbell ring and asked Malcolm to get it. His stepson let in Rose Trotter, the union's nurse organizer, followed by Gary Tuttle, Crystal and Mimi.

"Come in and get yourself a cup of coffee, breakfast will be in a few!" Lenny called. He was sharpening his favorite knife on a pumice stone when Rose poked her head in the kitchen.

"That's a beautiful knife, Lenny. You must be a hell of a cook."

"I am, if you count scrambled eggs and mac n' cheese gourmet food." He poured cups of coffee for the guests, then prepared the eggs. A few minutes later they were all seated around the table eating and exchanging remarks about Croesus.

Rose asked the other nurses if Lenny had warned them, the union campaign would be long and stressful. The administration was bound to come down on them hard. "You're going to have to be extra careful in your work. You need to cross your T's and dot your I's. You can't be five minutes late, and you can't be away from your unit for a moment except for approved break times or necessary errands."

"We're already under the gun all the time anyway!" said Mimi. "My supervisor tells me all the time I'm too slow to answer my patient's call light. But where's the staff to get it all done?"

Rose acknowledged she'd heard about the tracking devices. She said they were being used more and more in non-union facilities to bully the staff.

Taking a bite of her eggs, she saw Lenny spreading cream cheese on a bagel, then adding two slices of bacon and a few spoonfuls of eggs.

"I see you have a healthy appetite," she said.

Patience was about to make a comment when Gary grabbed a bagel in solidarity with his friend and smeared an extra thick layer of cream cheese on it, followed by some bacon. Malcolm gleefully followed suit, leaving Patience to roll her eyes and keep quiet.

Crystal talked about how the new GPS units were being used to dog their every movement and to write up the nurses if they doesn't answer a patient call light within two minutes.

"It's not fair!" she added. "If I'm hanging an IV medications I have to check the patient arm band against the medical record number on the med. Then I have to hang the drug, prep the site, check the intravenous site for inflammation. It's a whole complicated process just administering one I-V medication. But they're writing me up if I don't drop it to answer a patient who wants to know what time is lunch being served."

"Shouldn't the aides be answering the call lights?" said Rose.

"Not necessarily," said Crystal. "Now, a dispatcher asks the patient what he wants, and then, based on the answer, he either beeps the aide or the nurse."

"In *theory* the dispatcher *could* page the doctor first if it's a question for a physician. That's what they said would happen, but every time there's a medical question they call us nurses first and *we* have to page the doctor."

Rose made notes as she listened to the complaints, nodding her head and sometimes shaking it in disbelief.

"Here. Check this bad boy out," said Mimi, handing Rose the Croesus staffing assignment. She had copied her last shift's patient rating form along with the list of nurses, aides and clerk on duty.

Rose took one look at the paper and swore softly. She held it where Lenny could look at it with her. "This is an old dodge," she said. "It's a slick cover for making the workers work short."

Lenny ran his finger down the column with the staff assignment. "Everybody's got a number one by their name," he said.

"That's their *value,* according to the formula. Each employee can provide eight hours of patient care. Now look at the patient *acuity.*" Rose pointed to the list of patients, each of which had a numerical value. "That's a measure of how many nursing hours per shift a patient needs. A patient needing one-to-one nursing care would be an eight, for example."

"If I understand this," said Lenny, "if a nurse and an aide have the same *value,* it doesn't matter which one you staff them with. Is that right?"

"That's what the system allows," Rose agreed. "You could staff a nursing unit with six RNs and two aides, or six aides and two RNs. According to their formula, either staffing pattern would prove adequate care.

"But an aide or a clerk can't do a nurse's job!" said Mimi.

"And a nurse can do theirs!" said Crystal. "And we do. All the time!"

Gary Tuttle added that whenever they had no clerk, the nurse had to answer the phone and transcribe the doctor's orders.

"Or feed the patient when the aide was busy," Mimi added. "Or transport the patient. Or call pharmacy about a later delivery. Or... or anything!"

Asking for a copy of Mimi's staffing log, Rose said, "Okay, this is going to be our approach. That the new management is using a phony formula to short the staffing. Their system puts undo strain on the nurses and undermines the nurse's professional responsibilities by equating their contribution to patient care to an aide or a clerk."

"Not that the ancillary staff aren't super important," said Mimi. "It's just the fact that we can do all their jobs, and they can't do most of ours."

Lenny pointed out that the bogus staffing system hurt the patients as much as it hurt the nurses. So empowering the nurses to demand safe staffing made the patient care all that much better.

"I agree," Rose said. "The focus of our campaign should be that patient care suffers when nursing assignments go up. We're going to demand that James Madison staff their hospital according to the nurse-patient ratios approved by the California state legislature."

"That would be super!" said Mimi. "I read about that law. We need one in Pennsylvania for sure."

Rose said that was exactly why they needed to organize the nurses into a union; to bring more clout to the Pennsylvania legislature. She promised to rough out a flyer that afternoon and email it to the nurses and Lenny for them to revise and send back to her. "Let's plan to have it polished and ready to give out tomorrow morning."

The nurses agreed. Any old grievances or slights between nurses and aides or clerks or housekeeping now felt trivial. It was clear to everyone that they sank or swam together.

Gary held a cup of coffee between his hands and said, "I think we could all use some advice on the best way to approach our fellow nurses. The administration is going to be watching us like hawks when they hear about our efforts to join the union."

Rose gave the nurses a short but comprehensive explanation of how to talk to the rank and file about joining the union. Mimi and her coworkers vowed to begin making home visits that very day, believing many nurses would be home on a Sunday. They would incorporate many of the ideas about the harm done to workers and patients when there was no union in place from the flyer Lenny had already given out.

"When you're back at work, you have to keep the discussion confined to your break time," said Lenny. "They can cite you for using company time for organizing."

"Lenny's right," said Rose. "If the subject comes up while you are providing care, tell your coworker you want to talk about it during a break. Or suggest you hook up after work."

As the guests were packing up and getting ready to leave, Lenny and Rose agreed to bring the new flyer announcing the organizing campaign for the nurses to the hospital bright and early and hand it out at the main entrance, along with union cards for the nurses. Mimi hesitated a moment, realizing that that was the time she would really be in it. She would be committed. Her job would be on the line. She was scared and excited, and felt good to be part of it.

After the meeting was over, the dishes done and the house set to order, Lenny lay down for a nap, knowing he was in for a long night of work cleaning offices. With all of the excitement over the campaign for the nurses and the fight to keep the union, he thought he would never get the sleep. Picking up a book, history, he opened it and begin reading. But he couldn't focus, the words begin to blur, the sentences making no sense. He let the book drop into the bed, closed his eyes just for a minute and was soon fast asleep.

While Lenny slept, Malcolm penciled a crude sign that said LENNY SLEEPING and taped it to the bedroom door. Then he gathered some action figures on the table by the front window, a pillow and a blanket so that he could keep a look out the front window. After all, he was the man in charge.

THIRTY-THREE

While Lenny was sleeping, Gary and Mimi made their third visit of the afternoon. They sat in a cozy parlor room in a house in Northeast Philadelphia. The house was one of the block of buildings that had been sinking in the ground, having been built over soft landfill. Leslie, the owner of the house, was glad she had hung in and not abandoned the house in the early days. The house had stopped sinking, leaving her glad she had held onto her home.

"I just can't take this anymore," said Leslie. "The way they're treating me and the other nurses, it's just a rotten shame. I work like a dog, and the patients, they get it worse than me. I wouldn't send my cat to this hospital for treatment."

Leslie's girlfriend Karla agreed. "Things just seem to get worse and worse at the hospital. They want us to hurry up and care for the patients but they don't give us the staff that we need to do it! It's like blaming the victim, you know?"

Gary said it was the same in the ICU. Instead of two patients per nurse they were often getting three, so that on break time one nurse had to care for five or six critically ill patients. "It's not safe," said Gary. "For me or for the patients."

Mimi complained about the GPS unit they had to wear. "It's not right, they know where I am every second. They know when I go to the toilet! They know when I go to the pantry! Okay, I need to be at work, not run across to the cave and have a drink, but, come on, don't track my every footstep!"

Gary brought out the California regulations for nurse-patient ratios. He explained that the California legislature had set limits to the number of patients that a nurse could care for responsibly and safely. The hospitals had to abide by the limits if they were to stay in business.

"We want the same thing at James Madison," said Mimi. "We

want a union contract that sets limits to how many patients we have to take care of. It's a patient safety issue, no more, no less."

Leslie said she had heard about the California regulations and she thought they really needed them at James Madison, but her coworker was doubtful. "Won't that take away the staffing office's flexibility?" said Karla. "Some nurses call out on the weekend all the time. They have to have *some* way to fill the holes in the assignments."

Gary explained that protecting nurses from unsafe working conditions didn't 'tie the hands' of the staffing office, it just put a limit on how short they can make the nurses work.

"If nurses call out on the weekend, let them bring in agency nurses!" said Mimi. "And if it's a pattern, okay, demand a doctor's note. But don't make the nurse who came to work carry the load, that's no solution, that's punishing the good ones for the ones who call out!"

Karla asked what they needed to do to bring in the union. Mimi explained that they needed to fill out union cards, and they needed to give the cards to their friends and coworkers. "You have to careful, remember," said Mimi. "Don't let your head nurse see what you're doing. And you have to kind of get a feel for who you're talking to. There are some nurses who are tight with their boss, so you don't want to say too much to them. You can maybe, like, give an opinion, but you don't want to ask them to join a union, or tell them you're organizing with the union if you think that they're too tight with the boss."

Leslie and Karla signed union cards on the spot and took a bunch of them to take to work with them. Gary and Mimi left happy and encouraged. It looked like their union drive was heading for success.

<><><><><><>

With a giant mug of steaming black coffee on the table beside him, Detective Williams booted up his laptop and began viewing more of the video files the hospital security officer had given him, having been busy with another case the previous two days. Beginning with the camera covering the main entrance, he watched employees coming into the hospital, many of them wearing scrub suits or lab coats. Visitors with flowers or parcels of food came in, obtained a visitor's card at the information desk and went on in.

Williams was getting bored and his eyes were beginning to glaze over when a familiar face appeared in the doorway: Dante Soleil, the dialysis tech who had a beef with the dead man came walking in the front door wearing his ID badge and going right past the security guard. Williams made a note of the time on the time stamp imbedded in the image.

Now wide awake and intrigued, Williams smiled when he saw Louie Gordon entering the hospital fifteen minutes after Dante. Williams continued watching for another thirty minutes, but saw no other suspicious invididual coming into the hospital. There was no sign of the drug dealer Roland Weekes anywhere near the hospital.

Satisfied that he had solid evidence against Dante Soleil, his prime suspect, Williams switched to the video from Six North, where Louie had died. Joe West kept a camera trained on any area under reconstruction in order to discourage theft of equipment or vandalism.

The detective set the time for the same moment that Dante came through the main entrance. He watched and waited, waited and watched. But though he ran the video for over an hour, neither Dante nor Louie appeared on screen. Only the occasional security guard making his rounds disturbed the still life that was the entrance to Six North, the construction crew having quit work hours before.

Williams knew there were at least two stairwells opening onto the ward. He figured the victim and his killer had entered by that route, evading the security camera. Disappointed but convinced that Dante was the most likely suspect, he studied videos from other vantage points in the hospital. None of them showed anyone else of interest.

He was going to have to find more compelling evidence against Dante before he could make an arrest.

<><><><><><>

Waking from his nap, Lenny ate heartily and took his time reading the Sunday paper. Only after drinking his third cup of coffee and finishing the entire sports section did he call Gary Tuttle to learn how the visits with the nurses had gone. Gary told Lenny that their meetings had gone pretty well; that several of the nurses they had talked to were interested in joining the union. Some had reservations about being in the same union, but he thought the signs were good. Lenny told Gary he was encouraged, it was a good start of the campaign.

Asked what he was doing the rest of the day, Lenny told him he was going to take Malcolm to the zoo, eat cotton candy and act like a fool in front of the monkeys. Then he had to go to work again, cleaning the offices in Center City.

Gary hoped he had a good night at work and promised to talk to him the next day.

"I'll be at the hospital Monday morning giving out union literature," said Lenny. "I'll see you then."

"You won't get in any trouble, will you, coming back and all?"

"Nah, I'll stay on the public sidewalk, I won't be on hospital property, it'll be cool."

"That's good," said Gary. "Thank god we still live in a free country."

"Uh, yeah, good thing," said Lenny and hung up, not bothering to remind his friend that he was indeed free to sleep out under a bridge at night after he lost his home for being out of work.

THIRTY-FOUR

With the sun peeking out from behind the houses and trees, Lenny and Rose stood on the sidewalk along Germantown Avenue handing out union flyers. Workers getting out of cars or buses greeted Lenny with hugs and kisses, which surprised him. And when they saw the headline in the flyer – **SAVE THE UNION and RECRUIT THE NURSES!** they responded to the idea with exclamations such as "It's about time!" and "We need to all stick together!"

While most of the registered nurses who saw the flyer were warm to the idea, several were afraid to be seen taking a union pledge card. Rose assured them that a nurse inside the hospital would bring them one quietly and without their head nurse knowing.

Workers driving in to the parking lot stopped when they saw Lenny and called out to him asking for a copy of the flyer, creating a bottleneck at the main entrance.

Two security guards came rushing out of the hospital and marched up to the pair on the sidewalk. As the officers approached Lenny and Rose, workers stopped their cars in the entrance to see what would happen, while others on foot began to gather behind the leafleting pair.

Officer Jones, big and beefy and with a mean face, told Lenny he had to clear out or be arrested. When Lenny protested he was standing on a public sidewalk, Jones replied, "You're creating a disturbance. Look at all the cars backed up in the entrance. Employees can't get in to work. You got to pull out. *Now!*"

"You're the one creating the disturbance," said Lenny. "The workers were going in to work just fine until you showed up."

The workers behind Lenny called out in protest. "Leave 'em alone!" "They got their rights!" "This ain't Nazi Germany!"

Lenny wanted to spit in the man's face, but Rose stepped between them.

"Listen, officer," she said. "I can understand your concern about allowing free ingress and egress to the hospital. But we have a legal right to give out our materials."

"I got my orders. You have to go over across the street and give the shit out there!" said Jones.

"Who gave the orders?" said Lenny. "Was it Joe West?"

Just then a Philadelphia police car pulled up and came to a stop. Two officers emerged and approached the crowd.

"What's going on here?" said the first officer, addressing the security guards. Jones told him that the rabble-rousers were blocking traffic and making it impossible for workers to come to work. "I want them across the street the other side of Germantown Ave," said Jones.

Rose explained that they were just trying to give out informational material for thc union. She pointed out that they did have a right under law to distribute information. "Why can't we have one small piece of the sidewalk where people can come and take a literature?" She said

The police officer looked up and down the street. Lenny did not know it, but this officer had worked with Joe West in the past and didn't like him or his security team.

"All right. You two can stand over there away from the entrance to the hospital. If somebody wants to walk over and take material they can do so. But you can not stand at the entrance to the driveway. Understood?"

Rose looked at Lenny, Lenny looked at Rose. They shrugged their shoulders and started walking away from the driveway to a spot farther up the street but still in front of the hospital. Several of the workers walked with them to the alternate spot, where they grabbed many copies of the flyer and promised to give them out inside the hospital. As the workers walked past the security guards, their heads held high, they waived the flyers in the faces of the guards and headed through the entrance.

"God *damn*," said Lenny.

Rose smiled at Lenny. "God damn indeed."

<><><><><><>

Mimi was preparing her 8 am medications, and for once, was on time. With 12 patients under her care, she had come to work early and worked diligently to get all her ducks in a row. She had reviewed the doctor's orders on each chart, comparing the orders to the medication she was going to give out, and checking for procedures or tests that the patients might have to leave the ward to go to.

As she rolled her medication card into the hallway and took out her first dose of medication, she saw her head nurse walking toward her, grim faced and tight jawed. "Oh, boy," Mimi muttered to herself. "Here comes trouble."

"Mimi! A word."

The nursing supervisor took Mimi by the arm and led her into the employee lounge across from the nursing station. The two other nurses working with her were already seated there waiting.

Standing stiffly in front of the seated nurses, the supervisor told them she'd become aware of a scurrilous drive to bring the nurses into the nonprofessional union. "This would be a terrible thing to do to nursing. It lowers our professional status to that of the aide, or the housekeeper! A union is the worst thing that could happen to nursing and James Madison."

Sitting silently, the nurses looked down at their laps, not wanting to challenge the supervisor. Mimi felt a powerful urge to throw the words back at her boss's face. But Lenny and Rose had cautioned her not to discuss any union issues in front of any supervisor. There is no point in putting her face out so that she could be terminated for leading the union drive. So she kept quiet.

"Have you any questions for me?" said the supervisor.

The nurses kept quiet, following Mimi's lead.

"Very well. But if I hear so much as a *hint* that you are giving this idea any credibility, let me tell you, there will be consequences. Severe consequences!"

With that she turned and stalked out of the little lounge. As soon as she was gone the nurses looked at each other, not sure what to say. Standing and preparing to return to work, Mimi said, "You know what *I* think? I think if Mother Burgess is sending her skunks to put the fear of god in us, there must be something awfully good about joining the union."

'But Mimi," said one of her co-workers. "Wouldn't it be unprofessional of us to join the same union as the aides and the housekeepers?"

"What's *professional* about us caring for so many patients we can't provide half the care that they need?"

"How would a union help with staffing?" asked the other nurse.

"It would be in the contract. It would have nurse-patent ratios. It would make the hospital limit how many patients we'd be assigned to."

"Like in California?" asked the first.

"Yes! Like in California. It would be written into our contract, they couldn't give us so many patients."

The first nurse liked the idea of putting limits on her patient assignment. But she was still wary of joining a union. Especially the same one that organized the housekeepers, transporters, aides and other non-licensed workers.

When Mimi returned to her medication cart, she discovered one of the union flyers attacking the decertification campaign and calling on the nurses to join them on her cart. Looking around, she saw Little Mary cleaning a bed. Mary smiled and gave her a wink; Mimi showed her a thumbs up and went on with her tasks.

<><><><><><>

Martin Freely walked into the outer office of Human Resources and stopped dead in his track. He saw that the door to his own office was open, and there were two security guards going through his desk while Joe West stood watching them.

"What is the meaning of this?" Freely demanded, stepping into the room.

West looked at Freely, his face a mask of unconcern. "Let me have your ID badge," he said.

"What? What do you want my badge for?"

"You're terminated, as of today." West pointed at an empty cardboard box. "You can dump your personal things in that box and take them with you as you leave. I will monitor your selections to be sure you do not walk out with any hospital equipment."

"But this is absurd!" said Freely. "You can't do this to me!"

"If you have any complaints take them up with human resources," said West, smirking at his reference to the department that Freely had led until that very morning.

West stood impassively as a crestfallen Freely loaded pictures, paperweights, a few books and other personal items into the cardboard box. His souvenirs did not even fill one box.

"This will not be the end," said Freely.

He walked out of the office and continued to the main lobby of the hospital. From there he walked slowly out the door and descended the broad marble steps. Martin Freely almost lost his balance on the stairs, his head felt lightheaded and he was afraid he might pass out. But he regained his composure, cleared his head, and by the time he was at the bottom of the steps he was able to walk normally with head held high to the parking.

As Freely walked to his car, his cardboard box in hand and a security guard walking beside him, Lenny watched from his place on the sidewalk. He was surprised at first, but after a moment had a good idea what the termination was about. Freely had always tried to be fair in their negotiations with the union. Sometimes he sided with the union, sometimes he did not. But he had never been vindictive. Had never been a son of a bitch like Childress or Joe West.

Lenny felt a surge of sympathy for the man. At his age with the termination on his record it would not be easy to get another administrative job. Maybe it was better that way. Maybe Freely would take up some small business, like selling antiques, and find a life for himself. Knowing he would never see Martin Freely again, Lenny hoped things worked out for the man.

<><><><><><>

Throughout the hospital, nurses and aides, ward clerks and housekeepers were looking at each other in a new way. A circulating nurse in the operating room held the door open for the housekeeper, who was coming in with a rolling mop and bucket. Perhaps she would have done it anyway, but with the leaflet circulating widely, she felt a stronger sense of solidarity with the ancillary staff than she had in a long time.

In the dialysis unit Abrahm noticed the change in climate as well. He was wiping down a reclining chair, being sure there were no blood stains in the space where the chair folded, when a dialysis nurse said, "Hey, Abrahm, I'm going for coffee, you want something?" Usually the nurses went for their coffee, the housekeepers went for theirs, and the techs looked after themselves.

It was a new spirit being born out of the terror tactics and the disciplinary actions and terminations of the new regime. The greatest threat to the new bosses was cross-discipline unity. The bosses had known it for years. Now the workers were learning it, too.

As Mimi carried an IV antibiotic into her patient's room and hung it from a pole, her ear bud crackled to life. "The patient in seven-o-four needs assistance," said the dispatcher.

Mimi pressed the talk button. "What kind of assistance, I'm in the middle of hanging a medication."

"He has a question about a test he's scheduled for."

Mimi took a deep breath and held it, not wanting to curse in front of a patient or into a microphone the dispatcher could hear. Hell, she thought, they probably recorded everything the nurses said.

"Tell the patient I am giving a medication and I'll be with him as soon as I can. And for god's sake, don't mark me late if I don't rush down there. I need to prioritize my time. All right?"

"Room seven-o-four," the dispatcher repeated and hung up.

Shaking her head, Mimi decided to complete her current task, rather than drop it, go talk to a patient who could clearly wait, and then return to hook up the drug. It would be a mark against her, she knew, but she was not ready to let some computer program tell her how to organize her work.

Happy and scared, she scrubbed the hub of the patient's IV port, attached the antibiotic, opened the roller clamp and watched as it drip, drip, dripped into the chamber. Then she turned with a smile and headed for room four.

THIRTY-FIVE

After giving out all his leaflets and several union cards and saying good-bye to Rose, Lenny retired across the street to the Cave, where he ordered a breakfast of huevos rancheros and a large coffee. He was stirring the coffee, reflecting on what he'd done, when an uninvited guest sat down in the booth across from him.

"Lenny Moss. How's the union business these days?" Detective Williams signaled to the waitress for a cup of coffee, then looked back at Lenny.

"Actually, they're starting off pretty good. Considering the anti-labor climate we're living in, I heard a lot of positives from the workers this morning."

"I heard about the brush up you had with the hospital security. Those bozos think they're real cops. We have to pull them off people all the time, it's ridiculous."

Williams sipped the coffee placed in front of him. "But I need to talk about Louie Gordon. What have you found out about his murder?"

Lenny considered his options. He could hold back what he knew, but to what purpose? What would he gain? He was sure Louie's murder was linked to Joe West and the campaign to decertify the union. So helping Williams could help him beat back the attacks on the union.

He decided to be honest. To a point.

"Have you talked to the widow, Matilda?"

"Of course. She said she didn't know of anyone who wished to do Louie harm."

"That's what I'd expect her to say, to a cop. Did you know he signed his life insurance over to his dealer? A guy named Roland Weekes. He works out of the G-town car service down the street from the hospital."

"No, I didn't know that. That's interesting. It's a motive, I suppose, assuming Louie was in over his head and couldn't square his debt to his dealer."

"That's what I was thinking," said Lenny.

"How much of a scum bag is this guy?"

"About average. He's violent when he thinks he has to be. A lot of people are scared of him, including me. He's the reason I didn't want to take on the drug sales when I was a steward. I've got a family."

"I can't blame you, those bastards have no shame." Williams ordered a bagel with cream cheese and wrote down the dealer's name. "What else you got?"

"Your confidence in my investigative abilities is humbling." Lenny took a forkful of beans and eggs and enjoyed his status with the cop. "You should know that Louie's death might be connected with the hospital's campaign to decertify the union."

"Really? How so?"

"I heard from a reliable source..." Lenny paused, enjoying the annoyance on the detective's face when he held back Matilda'a name. Lenny knew that when the widow learned what Louie had done with his life insurance, she wasn't likely to testify about what her husband told her about the anti-union litearture that he saw. Especially with a drug dealer involved. "My source tells me that the day he died, Louie happened to see documents that linked the security department with the anti-union campaign."

"What exactly did he see?"

"My source isn't entirely clear on that. But I have a hunch he saw a security guard with the petitions that the bullshit 'independent committee' was going to circulate, before they showed up in the hospital."

"I get it. If evidence came to light that linked the administration to the campaign, it would sink their efforts to kill the union."

"And it could potentially open them up to a complaint with the

Labor Relations Board."

Williams nodded his head. "It sounds like a long shot, even for Joe West. I've got a simpler explanation for the murder."

Lenny mopped up some sauce with his toast. "Oh, yeah? What's that?"

"Dante Soleil." Williams enjoyed seeing Lenny's discomfort. "You didn't bother giving me his name last time we talked."

"I figured West already told you."

"Uh-huh. Soleil hated Louie for snitching on him. You didn't tell me anything about that." Lenny opened his mouth to object. "Don't bother to deny it, I saw the bullet hole in the tank at the hospital. He's got *no* alibi for the night of the shooting. And I saw him on the video coming into the hospital just before the victim... At a time he *wasn't on duty.*"

"Did you see him going into Six North? West always puts a camera on an area that's under construction, he worries about people stealing supplies or equipment."

"No. But I didn't see Louie going in, either. I didn't see *anybody.*"

"Louie probably took the stairs," said Lenny. "He didn't want to be seen."

When the detective opened his mouth to speak, it was Lenny's turn to interrupt, "I't's *not* Dante, I'm telling you. It's Joe West. Dante's got a temper, sure, but he's not a killer. Joe West and Croesus, *they're* the killers."

"That's your typical union crapola. You've got zero evidence against Joe West."

"Maybe not, but I will." Lenny dropped some money on the counter and drained the last of his coffee. "Don't bother calling me later, I'm turning off my phone and gonna sleep all day."

"You must be beat after cleaning offices down in Center City all night." said Williams, looking blasé.

Lenny stood by the booth looking down at Williams. "Huh. What d'ya know. You *are* a detective."

<><><><><><>

On the Seven South, Patience steered the x-ray machine down the hall. Passing the nursing station, an RN looked up and said, "Are you here for the chest x-ray on Mister Brimlow?"

Patience double-checked the request form. "That's the one, Ernest Brimlow. For an A-P chest."

"Let me help you, he's a big guy," said the nurse, rising from her chair.

As Patience steered the machine toward the patient's room, she was pleased to find that the nurses were seeing techs like her in a new way. How often did they volunteer to get up and help with an x-ray? Maybe there was hope for the hospital after all.

Finishing with the x-ray, Patience was steering her x-ray machine down the corridor when she spied Little Mary cleaning a discharge bed. Stopping outside the room, Patience asked if the housekeeper had a minute.

"Sure, baby, what you want?" said Mary, putting down her soapy rag.

"Well, it's sort of personal." She told Mary how Lenny had finished almost three years of college before dropping out and going to work in the hospital to help support his mother.

"You're thinking he oughta go back and finish up with school. Get a degree and all. Right?"

"I do. I know he loves his union work. But with a degree, he could do *more* for the union. Maybe serve in the union office. Or teach about unions in school."

"Oh, Lenny'd be a super teacher. He explains things so good, anybody can understand him. Even someone didn't get through high school like me."

"So you think it's a good idea."

"Sure I do! He don't need t' spend the rest of his life pushing a mop and fighting with Joe West. He can do a whole lot better for himself."

“Then you’ll support me on this:?’

Support you? I’m gonna knock some sense in his thick head first chance I get!”

“All right, thanks Mary. Just don’t hit him too hard, he has to use that head of his.”

Patience continued down the hall with her portable machine, pleased that friends like Little Mary wanted Lenny to succeed.

<><><><><><>

On another ward a nurse pressed the Talk button on her GPS unit to say, “I’m going to the bathroom to take a dump and change my sanitary napkin. Is that okay? Will I be written up if a patient needs me during my time at the toilet?”

There was a long silence in her ear.

The nurse asked her co-worker to listen for call lights and took a magazine into the staff toilet. She was damned sure no dispatcher was going to rush her time for her personal needs, time track or no time track.

THIRTY-SIX

With Mr. Mudge standing at the foot of the bed, Dr. Fahim instructed the respiratory therapist to remove the patient's breathing tube and switch Mrs. Mudge to oxygen by mask.

"We are giving her morphine in a continuous infusion," said the doctor. "She will feel comfortable and at peace, I assure you."

Making no comment, the husband looked around for a place to sit. Gary Tuttle hurriedly retrieved a chair from behind the nursing station and placed it at the bedside. Mr. Mudge slowly lowered himself into the chair, reached a trembling hand out to grasp the bedside rail, and rested his head a moment against the rail. Above his head, the tracing on the heart monitor slowly changed its shape, the complexes becoming fat and slow.

Gary thought it would not be very long before the husband needed a hospital bed himself.

<><><><><><>

Exhausted from his night shift cleaning offices and his confrontation with the hospital security, Lenny had dragged himself home and fallen heavily into his bed, waiting for sleep to wipe out all the troubles of the day. But sleep would not come. Something was nagging at him. Something about the case, not the union. It was there, a wisp of a thought, teasing him and staying just out of reach.

He went over the conversation with Detective Williams once more. Louie's cryptic text message; the drug dealer recipient of Louie's insurance money; how Louie showed up in the video entering the hospital but not going into Six North. Lenny knew West kept a camera trained on any construction site. Louie must have taken the stairs, especially if he was going to the site to buy some weed.

But what if he *hadn't* taken the stairs?

What if Louie *did* enter the ward under construction by the regular doors? Lenny knew the man was careless about his illegal activities; that was why he was always calling Lenny to bail him out of a jam. So if Louie acted like the dumb ass he usually was, the failure of the video to show him entering the area could only mean one thing: *somebody had doctored the tapes.*

It was a long shot, he knew; an idea that would almost certainly come to nothing. But what could it hurt to view the video carefully with Williams? He sent the detective a text asking him to bring a copy of the video to Lenny's house around five, they would watch it together.

Sensing no more wisps swirling in the depths of his mind, Lenny gratefully closed his eyes and was instantly asleep.

Nobody heard his snoring.

<><><><><><>

While Mr. Mudge sat alone in the waiting room, Gary asked Patty, another ICU nurse who had worked at James Madison for twenty years, to help him with the postmortem care. Usually after a death he would clean the body with an aide, but he wanted to get a sense of where the other nurse stood on the union issue.

Gently running a soapy washrag over the body, Gary asked Patty what she thought of the nurses joining the union.

Patty said, "Jeez, Gary, I never thought nurses would end up like Teamsters. I don't know, it kind of goes against how I've always thought of myself, you know?"

"I pretty much thought the same thing when I was in nursing school," said Gary. "But the way they're assigning us three patients at a time, I don't see anyone else standing up to the administration. Do you?"

"I guess not." As they patted the body dry, Patty asked about the nurse-patient ratios discussed in the flyer. Gary explained that the California nurses' union had convinced the state legislature to make the staffing limitations law. Patty said, "Why don't we go that way? Why don't we ask the city council to pass a motion or something?"

"Because a nurses' union is the only body with resources to put that kind of campaign together. You know the hospital will fight it tooth and nail."

"Oh, I see what you mean. Crap." She removed the wet sheet beneath the body and rolled out the white plastic morgue sheet. "I guess we need to go along with the union for our patient's sake. Is that it?"

"It certainly looks that way to me," said Gary.

Patty tied the toe tag around the big toe, checking to be sure the name matched the name on the dead woman's wrist band. "Remember that time the funeral home took the wrong body?" said Patty. "Now *that* was embarrassing."

"It was before my time," said Gary. He brushed the hair and lifted the head so that Patty could tie it back with a hair band.

"It's funny," said Patty. "I always want to put a little rouge and some lipstick on a remains like her. But I figure that kind of insults the funeral home. That's their job, isn't it?"

Gary leaned back and appraised the dead woman's face. "I think it would be nice."

Patty took out the deceased's makeup kit and applied just a little rouge to the cheeks and a hint of lipstick.

Satisfied, they wrapped the plastic sheet around the body, leaving the face exposed. Then they laid a crisp white sheet over the body, making it neat and square across the bed.

Patty removed the dirty linen and wash basin while Gary went to bring the husband back for one last look at his wife.

<><><><><><>

Shortly after the body had been taken to the morgue and Mr. Mudge had left the ICU, the ward clerk called out to Gary. "Mister Tuttle! The ER's on the phone, they want to give you report on your new patient."

Gary complained the empty bed was not even clean yet.

"What do you want me to tell the ER?" said the clerk.

"Tell them I will call for report as soon as the bed is ready."

Five minutes later, as the housekeeper was wiping down the empty bed, the nursing supervisor came into the ICU. Approaching Gary, she said, "Mr. Tuttle. What's this I hear that you refused to take report on an ER patient?"

"What are you talking about?" said Gary "I didn't refuse an admission."

"That's not what the ER nurse told me." The supervisor held out a form with her handwritten note documenting the incident. "I want you to take report right away or there will be serious consequences."

"But the bed isn't even clean yet!" said Gary, pointing at the housekeeper wiping down the bed.

"That's okay. By the time the ER nurse has the patient packed up and in the elevator the bed will be dry and you can put on fresh linen."

"What about my lunch break? By the time the new patient arrives it will be lunch time. And this is my third patient."

"I will put you down for one hour of overtime," said the supervisor. "You can grab something to eat later and take it in the back room."

"I can't have my lunch break? I need to put my feet up once during a twelve-hour shift."

"Work out your lunch arrangement with the other nurses, but get the new patient up here."

The supervisor walked away before Gary could say another word.

THIRTY-SEVEN

Dr. Reichart stood at the head of the conference table, his angry face reflected in the gloss of the polished teak table. "Croesus does not tolerate insubordination or defamation," he said, stabbing the latest union flyer with a finger. "You will root out the perpetrators and terminate them on the spot. I have asked Legal to advise us on our rights to sue the union and the individuals involved for slander and defamation."

He looked down at a dark haired gentleman in a pinstriped suit and blood red tie seated beside him. The gentleman cleared his throat.

"I have reviewed recent Supreme Court rulings on defamation of character. While it is premature to assert there is no case to be made, I must caution everyone that criticism of an institution or of an immediate supervisor is not a prima facie case of slander, especially if there are any grounds for the accusations."

"Are you telling me that these lies about Croesus being the 'hidden hand' behind the committee to save James Madison cannot be challenged in court?"

"Of course they can be challenged. And I will challenge them if you so order me to do so. But if the union comes up with any evidence that supports their assertions, we will not only lose the case, we will be liable for court costs."

"And we'll look like chumps in the media," said Slocum. "The union would love us to take them to court. It gives them a bully pulpit where they can spew their lefty rhetoric."

Red faced and agitated, Miss Burgess held a hand up, finger pointed to the ceiling. "We are facing a rebellion among the nurses. We *must* do something immediately to keep our girls in line."

"Is it really that bad?" asked Reichart.

"I'm afraid it is. I have reports from the dispatchers that nurses are openly defying orders to attend to a patient."

"Fire them! Fire them at once!"

"That was my first reaction, of course. But the nurses are complaining that they aren't being allowed to go to the toilet. One nurse announced to the dispatcher she was going to the bathroom to change her sanitary napkin and she didn't want to be reprimanded for taking more than five minutes to answer a call light."

"Unprofessional and insubordinate," said Slocum."

"Another nurse told dispatch she was discussing a case with a doctor and that it was rude to break it off just to run down to answer a question that could wait for five minutes."

Reichart said he understood the new tracking and dispatch system would take some getting used to. He told Miss Burgess that the nurses must maintain their professional decorum and act like ladies, not truck drivers.

The President turned his attention to the decertification issue. He said he wanted assurances that the petition to decertify the union would succeed. Mister Nance, the acting head of Human Resources, told him he believed there was good support for the campaign, but he couldn't peer too deeply into the labor pool to extract more accurate information, it would look too much like meddling.

"Very well," said Reichart. "We will hold off the legal challenge against the goddamned union for the moment." He turned to Joe West and asked why the people handing out the union flyers hadn't been handcuffed and taken away. West explained the local police officer had negotiated a small spot on the sidewalk where they could stand, so long as they did not disrupt pedestrian through-fare.

"You can't get rid of them entirely?"

"No, sir. But they have been ordered to stay well away from the drive leading into the main entrance. And they cannot stand at the entrance itself. They're pretty much isolated where they are."

Reichart was not satisfied; he wanted the union representatives arrested. "Why don't you start a fight with one of them and then arrest them for disorderly conduct?"

West paused. "I'm familiar with that approach, of course. Unfortunately, they always have sympathizers in the area with cell phones that can capture video. Any time our security people approach them, they whip out their cameras and record us."

Miss Burgess pointed out that the guidelines for safe nurse-patient ratios had been widely published. "Quoting those numbers and comparing them to our numbers, assuming the report is accurate, can't be considered libelous," she said. "The recommendations have been published by several professional organizations."

Reichart was growing increasingly angry. "You have to make it clear that ratios are fine in an ideal world, but we don't live in an ideal world. We live in a time of unprecedented competition and diminishing resources. The government keeps cutting Medicare and Medicaid, the private insurance companies take sixty, ninety, a hundred twenty days to pay a bill, *if* they pay it at all. Our girls must be made to see that we will only be able to provide the staffing levels they want when the institution establishes a solid financial foundation."

He instructed Miss Burgess to order all the head nurses to meet with their employees and make his remarks clear to them. The future was bright if everyone pulled together. If they went ahead and voted for the nurses' union, they had no future, the hospital would be out of business. Reichart instructed West to see that his guards kept on watching for anyone with a union flyer on their person and to fire them on the spot if they did.

THIRTY-EIGHT

Norman Childress stood in front of the blackboard in a classroom as the housekeeping staff filed into the room. Once the last worker was seated, he thanked them for coming to the emergency meeting while the supervisors handed out a paper. The workers looked over the handout while the boss went on talking.

"I know there have been a lot of rumors about the new administration and about changes at our facility," Childress said. "I'm here to set the record straight. The committee that has proposed dropping the union is an *independent group of employees.* They are dissatisfied with how the union treats them, for whatever the reason, I don't know why and I don't frankly care. But that is their feeling and we must respect it."

He picked up a copy of his memo and held it up where all could see it. "It is imperative that you read this handout and that you think long and hard about what it says. The new owners of this facility are serious about righting the ship and setting us on a strong fiscal path. This right-sizing will mean sacrifices from all of us, in every department. But it is the *only* way to keep the hospital in business, and all of you employed."

Abrahm raised his hand. "Mister Childress. What does paper mean, Croesus will make housekeeping department private if union is not decertified? Is outside company you are talking about?"

"I have it on good authority that senior management has drawn up plans to outsource several departments, including laundry and housekeeping. If the union remains and continues to represent the employees, the only way to keep the hospital solvent is for them to switch several services to private companies."

Little Mary stood up. "So if we vote to keep the union, we're all out of a job. That's what you sayin', isn't it?"

"Keeping the union will result in many, if not all of you losing your jobs. A private contractor will take over responsibilities for cleaning the hospital. That company will be free to hire anyone they choose."

"That's blackmail!" cried Mary. "That ain't even legal!" Murmurs of agreement rose from the crowd.

"There is no guarantee that the private contractor coming in will hire any one of you. They may prefer to begin with new faces they can train appropriately."

"We lose the union, we lose our rights!" she said. "We lose our respect! We got to keep the union here, no matter what!"

Childress glared at Mary but made no effort to challenge her. He ended his remarks by repeating that the laundry would be sent out to a private firm that was not unionized if the union remained in place. He ended by saying that now was not the time to slack off just because the work was hard; now was the time to redouble their efforts and show Croesus that they could get the job done.

When the meeting was over, several of the housekeepers gathered outside the office. A few were afraid if they didn't sign the decertification petition and they kept the union, the hospital would do good on its threat to outsource the whole department. Little Mary swore a long streak. "I ain't givin' in to no blackmail! I'll go out fighting before I'll beg for a job from that son of a bitch!"

That raised smiles among several co-workers. But still they were afraid. Seeing unemployment staring them in the face, several would rather swallow the bitter pill of giving up the union rather than give up their position at James Madison.

<><><><><>

The same nursing supervisor who had threatened Gary to take a report on a patient from the ER returned to the ICU, this time all smiles and warm greetings. She called the four RNs to the nursing station. "I know these are difficult times for all of us," she said.

"You have four nurses caring for ten patients. It is not the ideal situation, but it is a necessary one."

She went on to explain that the new administration had inherited a facility that had been losing a million dollars a week. "No business can continue to operate with that business model. It simply cannot be sustained. So we are all of us tightening our belts and doing what we have to do to right the ship and steer us back into profitable waters."

"Why can't I get my vacation time approved," asked another nurse. "I've submitted three different dates and the head nurse turned them all down!"

The supervisor reiterated that difficult financial times meant everyone had to make sacrifices. "We can't afford to pay overtime or to hire any more agency nurses," she said. "But the bottom line is getting better every day. We're shortening our length of stay – that saves us a big pool of money. And the new team is launching new procedures that will bring in additional revenues."

Patty asked how soon they could go back to assigning no more than two patients per nurse. The supervisor assured her that was their number one, absolute first priority. Gary could see that his coworker was troubled by the supervisor's remarks, but he couldn't tell if she had been swayed by them or not.

"The important thing to keep in mind is that a union for nurses would sink this hospital, and then we would all be out of work."

"How would that happen?" asked Gary.

"By insisting on those artificial nurse-patient ratios, for one. We cannot afford them, the reimbursement rates are sinking, Medicare and Medicaid are cutting back what they pay us. We are no longer paid for extended stays due to hospital acquired infections, you all know about that problem."

The nurses had been drilled by Dr. Augenello many times about the cost to the hospital *and* to the patient when they developed an infection while in the hospital.

"Besides the staffing ratios, a nurse's union would tie up our management team with a long list of restrictions and provisos. It would mean constant fighting with management. We *must* have flexibility to make the best, most efficient use of our employees. That's why we hope the petition to decertify the nonprofessional union succeeds, it will be a huge economic gain for James Madison."

She ended by assuring the nurses that as soon as the hospital's economic fortunes turned around under the new programs, the patient assignments would become easier and management would be much more liberal granting time off for vacations.

<><><><><><>

Detective Williams inserted the thumbnail drive into Lenny's laptop and ran the first video clip from the hospital surveillance program. The video showed a steady stream of workers of all types straggling in to begin their shift.

"There's a shot of Louie coming in through the main entrance at ten-seventeen pm," said Williams. "You can see the time stamp on the lower right section of the image.

"But he wasn't scheduled to work that late, was he?"

"No, his shift ended at four. He had no official reason to be in the hospital."

They watched several more workers come in, then the evening shift began to make their way home.

The video switched to an image of the entrance to Six North. Lenny could see the KEEP OUT sign clearly posted on the door.

"There's the entrance to the crime scene. As you can see, nothing happens for long stretches of time," said Williams.

"The workmen have gone home for the day."

"That's right, they quit at seven. A security guard did a walk-through at nine pm. I checked, that's part of his regularly scheduled rounds."

"Got ya."

"But if you fast forward to the time around when Louie died, there is no image of anyone going in or out of the ward."

"You think Louie used the stairwell," said Lenny.

"I would if *I* were planning on engaging in an illegal enterprise."

"So would I, but I'm not Louie. He was always pretty damn careless in his extra-curricular activities around the hospital. That's why I ended up having to defend him so many times." Lenny asked Williams to rewind the tape of Six North to before Louie would have died and to play it in slow motion.

"What do you think you'll see in slow mo that's not visible in the regular play mode? Nobody came through, the image is static the whole time."

Lenny leaned closer to the computer screen and studied the time stamp in the image. With each six frames, the counter advanced one second. He folded his hands beneath his chin, squinted and watched.

"Stop it there!"

Williams hit the pause button.

"What is it? I don't see anything," said Williams.

"Look at the time stamp. You see the time?"

"Yeah. So?"

"Now go back slowly."

Williams ran the tape backward. At one point Lenny had him go back one frame at a time, which was exceedingly slow. All of a sudden, the time changed back by twenty-eight seconds – all between two single frames.

"I'll be a monkey's uncle," said Williams. "The bastard doctored the tape."

THIRTY-NINE

Lenny sat back from the computer screen and absorbed what he and Williams had discovered. He said he had known it was a long shot, looking for a break in the time stamp on the video. But he'd seen Louie do a lot of stupid things over the years, oblivious to the unnecessary risks he was taking. His guess that Louie had acted true to form paid off. The man had walked into the construction site through the main doorway without thinking about the video camera watching the construction site.

Lenny ran the tape forward again. A few minutes after the first gap, a second loss of video appeared, this one lasting fifty-five seconds. They watched for another twenty minutes, but there were no more breaks in the time record.

"Okay," said Williams. "It looks like there was footage of Louie and his killer on the tape entering the ward. Whoever carried out the murder probably left by the stairwell and didn't have to erase any more."

"Could be he didn't go in there planning on killing Louie."

"Too early to tell, we don't have enough information," said Williams.

Lenny suggested there might be a way to find the missing data. If the computer didn't over-write the relevant section on the hard drive, the data would still be there. Williams promised to check that possibility out with his IT specialist right away.

"You know what bothers me the most?," said Lenny. "Let's say somebody followed Louie into the construction area. Let's say he gives the guy the doctored weed with the strychnine in it, and he watches as Louie goes into the asthma attack."

"He's cold-blooded, no doubt about that."

"Louie would use his inhaler, but it doesn't give him any relief. So why doesn't he run for help to the nursing station across the way, where there are nurses and doctors and a working phone."

"Like I said, cold-blooded. The killer must have restrained Louie while he was in the midst of the asthma attack."

"That's what I was thinking," said Lenny. "Maybe he put him in a choke hold to keep him in that room. Choking him when he's already gasping for breath. Does that sound like anybody we know?"

Williams looked into Lenny's eyes. He didn't need to be a mind reader to know where Lenny was going. "Unfortunately, we can't arrest Joe West on the basis of his personality. We need evidence. We need cold, hard facts."

"Then let's get them. Let's nail the bastard. Find the original video footage and we have West."

Williams stopped the video and was about to eject his thumbnail drive when Lenny asked him to rewind the video to where Louie first entered the hospital through the main entrance. He was hoping the video would show Joe West coming in around the same time.

"There's no sign of West coming in," said Williams. "Waste of time."

"Humor me. I know a lot of the staff. Maybe I'll spot somebody you wouldn't pick up on."

Williams ran the video showing employees and visitors coming into the building. Watching closely, they scrutinized each figure coming in the door. Nobody was obviously out of place, except Dante, who entered the hospital fifteen minutes before Louie.

"You think Dante killed Louie, don't you? You heard how Louie dimed on Dante about the gun going off in dialysis and you right away went after him. Didn't you?"

"Dante Soleil doesn't work that late, I checked his schedule," said Williams.

Lenny glared at the detective. "I'm not surprised you're looking at him, I know you interviewed him."

"Hey, I go where the evidence leads me. When I asked him what he was doing the night Louie was killed he gave me some bullshit story about being home alone watching 'the game'. Like he couldn't record it and watch it the next day."

"Listen, detective. If I'm going to share my information with you, you've got to keep me in the loop, too. This is supposed to be a two-way street, remember?"

"Don't get your bowels in an uproar, I was going to tell you, I just haven't been able to get around to see you is all. I think that-"

Son of a bitch!" Lenny suddenly called out. "Will you look at that?" He rewound the video and froze it on the image of a burly hospital security guard coming through the main entrance a few minutes after Louie. "I know that bastard. He's officer Jones, Joe West's main enforcer. He's been following me with a video camera recording my movements. He even tried to spark a confrontation and arrest me out on the sidewalk the other day when I was giving out union literature."

"Okay, he's an enforcer for Joe West. That doesn't connect him to Louie."

"No, but I remember Louie telling me last year when he was in trouble over that shot that was fired in the dialysis unit, he thought about making a run for it, but the guard watching over him was as big as a lineman for the Eagles. And as mean. I bet it was that guy."

"Like I said, he's an enforcer for West."

"What else does he enforce? Is he deep into the drug trade? Is he fronting the decertification campaign for West? We know the administration is behind it. And we know Louie saw something that one of the guards was holding that linked the anti-union campaign to the hospital administration."

Williams took notes on all of Lenny's observations. "I don't think it's enough to get a search warrant for his phone. But I can certainly look into his credit rating. Any unexplained deposits, big purchases, that sort of thing."

"Good. I'll talk to a friend in the security department, see what he knows."

Williams left, leaving Lenny feeling for the first time they might actually solve this bitch of a case.

<><><><><><>

After doing the laundry and hanging it out in the backyard to dry, Lenny drove to the hospital, hoping his luck would be good. It was. His friend Sandy, the old security guard, was in the little electric kart touring the parking lots as the day shift workers on an 8 hour tour were going home. He waved to the guard, who aimed his vehicle for Germantown Ave and came to a stop by the sidewalk.

"Lenny! So good to see you. Man, it hurt me so bad, hearing Joe West done busted you. You okay?"

"Yeah, I'm fine. Moose got me a temporary job cleaning offices in Cener City. It's a lot easier than working in this hole, I'll say that."

"So you're gettin' to like working the private sector."

"I didn't say that! No, the union filed an appeal. I think I'll get my job back, it's just a matter of time."

"I sure hope so. The place is kinda boring without you around."

Lenny asked Sandy if he knew who handled the video equipment in the security department. The old guard said all the editing and repairs were done by a young guard named Winterbottom.

"*Winterbottom?* What the hell kind of a name is that?" said Lenny.

"Hell, I don't know, that's what his daddy was called, so that's his name." Sandy went on to say that the young fellow had big dreams in law enforcement. "Boy wants t' get into the FBI. He's taking all kinds a' forensic courses and such at Temple. He's hoping the security job is just a temporary stop on his way to Pennsylvania Avenue."

"Okay, thanks." As Sandy started to turn his cart around, Lenny stopped him to ask would he find out if Officer Jones was on duty the night Louie was killed.

"Sure I can do that. You're thinkin' he was in on it?"

"I saw him on the video going into Six North right after Louie did."

"I always knew that man was a son of a bitch. Just didn't know how much a one he was." Sandy put the cart in gear one more time. "What you gonna do with the information you collectin'?"

"I'm working with a Philly detective. He's carrying most of the work."

Sandy shook his head, smiling broadly. "That's be Detectve Williams. I remember when you trusted that man 'bout as far as you could throw him. I never would've thought I'd see the day you helping the po-lice do their work."

"Yeah, well, my dad used to say, hard line, flexible tactics."

"Smart man, your daddy. Smart man."

<><><><><><>

That night, while Patience was sitting in bed rubbing lotion on her legs, Lenny took a squirt and began rubbing it into her foot. She leaned back in the bed, and closed her eyes, enjoying the message.

"Have you thought about what would happen if you didn't go back to the hospital?" she said.

Lenny's hands froze for a few seconds. "What do you mean?"

Opening her eyes, she looked at her husband with the deepest love and sympathy. "I mean, there's no guarantee you'll win the arbitration. You've told me a million times, it's always a crap shoot, you can never be sure how it will turn out."

Lenny sat beside her, leaning against the head board.

"I thought about it. Once. Then I put it out of my mind."

"I know. I understand. You've put practically your whole life into that job. The union work, I mean. It would be horrible if you could never go back there to work. But I think you should be prepared for the worst, just in case it happens."

"Like going into the doctor's office afraid he's going to say it's cancer."

"But it's not *cancer*. It *feels* like a death sentence, but it's not. It really isn't."

"Well I'll still be *alive,* more or less."

"Lenny! How many times have you told a worker who was fired they have options. They have opporltunities they didn't even think about when they were stuck in their job. Like going back to school."

"I know..."

"You could finally finish your college degree. You could get the degree and work for the union. You could be a *paid* organizer and stop giving all your time away for free."

"We don't have the money right now for college."

"Then take a couple of courses on line, they're very inexpensive. Take your time with it."

Lenny pulled a book from the pile on his bedside table. "I really don't want to think about it. Not now. Now I have to put everything I have into the fight to save the union. But after that, when it's time to prepare my case for the arbitration, then I'll think about what if."

Patience kissed him tenderly, then settled down into the bed.

"You going to read awhile?"

"Yeah, I'm not sleepy."

"'Kay. Good night."

She switched off the reading light on her side of the bed, turned away from him and closed his eyes, while Lenny sat for a long time thinking about the unthinkable, and trying to imagine himself in a sports coat and tie traveling around Pennsylvania organizing the union.

FORTY

On Tuesday morning Lenny was parking his car a block from the hospital when a Lincoln Town Car with a battered rear bumper and smokey windows pulled up beside him. The passenger side window lowered, revealing Roland Weekes in the driver's seat.

"Lenny Moss," said Weekes. "I hear you been sticking your nose into other people's business." If ever a character looked like a B movie extra playing the muscle, it was Roland Weekes. From the goatee and sideburns to the small, weasel eyes and the clinging knit shirt, he was every bit the thug he was purported to be.

"I don't know what you mean, Weekes. I'm a union steward. I look after my people, what's it to you?"

Weekes put the transmission in park, opened the door and stepped out. Lenny was glad he had the Lincoln between them, he knew the man was fond of carving letters in the skin of his victims.

"My boys say you've been stepping outside your area. Asking about things that don't concern you."

"You've got me confused with somebody else. The police are looking into things that happened at the hospital. Me, I'm concerned about the union."

"That's good, Moss. See that you keep it that way. I'd hate to see anything unpleasant happen to your family. The kiddies seem like such nice little people. They should grow up to like their mommy and daddy. Don't you think?"

Lenny felt something snap inside him. He locked his car door and walked up to the passenger side of Weekes's car, put his two strong hands on the window sill, bent down so the drug dealer could see his face clearly and said, "Oh, yeah? Well lemme tell *you* something, dirt ball. I've got a lot of friends in that hospital. A *lot*. And they've all got guns. In fact, one of 'em has a Mongolian bow and arrow he uses to hunt wild animals. At night. It's totally silent. You don't here any shot or clap, you just feel the arrow when it pierces your neck and sticks out the other side."

Turning away before Weekes could respond, Lenny walked toward the hospital, not daring to look back, he didn't want the drug dealer to see how scared he was. That his hands were trembling and he was bathed in sweat. But at the same time he was happy, knowing his threat had not been an idle one, and hoping his friends would never have to make good on the promise.

Drug dealers were the worst. He wished he didn't have to deal with them. But drugs were part of the investigation.

Reaching the hospital, Lenny found Rose standing under a threatening sky waiting for him. She asked how he was doing. He told her okay and left it at that.

They gave out leaflets and union information without any major incidents, having stayed in their circumscribed space. Several workers stopped to talk to Lenny, giving him words of encouragement and expressing confidence he would be back on the job soon, "with full back pay."

Lenny was about to unlock his car when Detective Williams pulled up in his unmarked police car and stepped out.

"Like to join me for coffee?" Williams said.

"If you're buying."

They walked down the street to a little café with seating on the sidewalk. Lenny ordered a double shot Americano, Williams had coffee, black. Once settled outside, the detective told Lenny he had his computer expert examine the hard drive in the security office. Unfortunately, the videos are over-written every seventy-two hours. There was no way to capture the missing data.

Lenny stirred two spoons of sugar into his coffee, blew on the mug and took a first sip. "I figured that would be the case. So I talked to a contact in the security department. He tells me the man who manages their computer systems is a young guy named Winterbottom."

Williams took out a notepad and began writing.

"Winterbottom is young. He's new and he's ambitious. In fact, he has dreams of joining the FBI." Williams looked up a this news, his face brightening. "Maybe if you lean on the man, he'll give up whatever he knows."

"So you don't think Joe West did the erasing himself."

"It's possible. But usually West has somebody else do his dirty work. That gives him that old plausible deniability angle."

"Even so," said Williams, "trusting somebody new with that kind of assignment would be awful risky. Especially someone who has aspirations for something greater."

"Greater, maybe, but not necessarily more honest."

Williams admitted he agreed with Lenny's assessment of the FBI's integrity. He promised to take Winterbottom away from the department and interrogate him properly.

"Oh, and you might as well know, I looked at the financials for that guard we saw, Jones. His income does look to be higher than it should be. There's no giant deposit that would raise a red flag, but the numbers are suspicious."

"Is he married? Does he have a wife bringing in income?"

"No. As a matter of fact, he spends a fair amount of his hard earned wages in massage parlors and strip clubs. By itself, it's not incriminating. But I don't see where he gets the extra money?"

"Yeah, those places can cost you an arm and a leg, or worse," said Lenny. "Not that I ever frequent them, I'm just going by what I hear."

Williams didn't bother to challenge Lenny on the remark. He said he was going to apply to a judge for a search warrant for the guard's car, workplace locker, home, and bank deposit box. "I'm telling the judge you have an anonymous source who gave you the information about Officer Jones. Your source is reliable, I take it."

"My source is solid. You can take the information to the bank."

"And he'd make a good witness at a trial?"

Lenny hesitated. He was reasonably sure that once Louie's

widow found out he'd signed away his life insurance she would be unwilling to testify to what she'd heard him say about the hospital connection to the decertification campaign, if only out of spite. But Lenny needed Williams to get the search warrant. "My source is *very upset* about Louie's death, that much I can guarantee. I think I can safely say that my source wants whoever killed Louie to be brought to justice."

"All right, that's good. I'll make reference to a reliable anonymous source inside the hospital. That, plus the video footage and the guard's history with Louie should get me the search warrant."

Williams got up and headed for the hospital to look for Officer Winterbottom, leaving Lenny to pay the bill and to reflect on the slow wheels of justice creaking along over a rusty track.

<><><><><><>

Mimi looked at the breakfast tray of uneaten eggs, bacon, toast and oatmeal on the patient's bedside table. "Are you feeling sick to your stomach, Mrs. Marshall?"

"No, I'm not sick, I'm hungry! The doctor sent me for a test this morning, and now my breakfast's cold. Can you heat it up for me?"

Mimi was about to explain that the hospital had a new policy, implemented by Croesus, that the nurses were no longer allowed to heat up a tray of food for a patient because *one* patient *one time* sued the hospital claiming his mouth had been scalded from hot-hot food heated by a nurse's aide.

The nurses were supposed to go down to the kitchen - *in the basement* - and bring back a new tray of hot food. But by now the breakfast line would be closed, there wouldn't *be* any breakfast left. And with all the tasks she and the aide had to do that morning, no way could she leave the ward and pick up a tray for a patient.

As she opened her mouth to speak, the nurse felt the anger and resentment that had been building for months come bubbling up.

How dare the administration make her serve her patients cold food? How dare they!

"I'll warm it up for you, Mrs. Marshall, it'll only take a minute."

Mimi carried the tray to the little pantry, put the plates in the microwave and heated them up. Then she tested them with her finger to be sure they weren't *too* hot.

One of the aides walking by saw what Mimi was doing and asked if she wouldn't get in trouble for breaking the new rule. Mimi cursed the rule and cursed the bosses. "I'm putting *my* patient first and to hell with the new rules. I'm getting her a hot breakfast, and I don't care who knows it!"

In minutes all the nursing staff knew about Mimi's rebellion. Passing her in the hall or meeting her at the nursing station, the other nurses congratulated her on her bold initiative, though they confessed they weren't sure they would have the nerve to follow suit.

"Aren't you afraid of being written up?" said Patty, one of Mimi's coworker.

"Sure I'm scared. I'm scared of losing my job, my husband was laid off. But I'm so damn tired of being pushed around and not being able to care for my patients the way I was trained to do."

"I hear you, Mimi. I just worry for your sake the head nurse will hear about it and find something that really does put your license in jeopardy."

"You mean, like letting an elderly patient fall out of bed and break her hip?"

"Yes. That's exactly what I mean."

"Fine. Let them call me up and review my license. I still say there was a reason Mrs. Mudge got confused and climbed over the side rails, and I'm going to find out what it is if it kills me." She coiled her stethoscope around her neck, adding, "This is why we need to build the damn union. Let's let nursing stand for something!"

<><><><><><>

Sandy stepped into the security office and smiled sweetly at the secretary, who smiled back, always happy to see the friendly old guard, who never tried to hit on her or look down her blouse. Sandy asked if he could look at last week's schedule. "I swear I thought I got some overtime comin' to me, but I might be mixed up 'bout when I worked."

The secretary pulled the schedule and laid it out for Sandy to review. It listed all the security officers and showed who was on duty each day and each shift with an X in the time slot. Sandy took out a pocket calendar and pretended to look over his own schedule. Seeing that the secretary was not looking his way, the old guard ran his finger along the timeline for Officer Jones. As he and Lenny suspected, Jones was not working the 4-12 shift the day Louie died. In fact, he wasn't supposed to be in the building at all.

"Son of a pup," he muttered to himself. "We got ourselves a killer."

As soon as he was out of sight of the security office, Sandy took out his cell phone and called Lenny to tell him what he'd found. Lenny promised to tell Detective Williams right away.

"Po-lice should be able to get a search warrant for Jones with what you've got so far," said Sandy. "There's no tellin' what kind of dirt they'll find. Drug sales. Murder. Maybe even a connection to Joe West."

"I'm hoping we can find real evidence that West was behind the decertification campaign. If we get that, their campaign will fall apart."

Sandy was about to hang up when Lenny said, "Listen, I know this is asking a lot, but is there any way you could get the names of the people who were at Louie's code? I'd like to get a better picture of what went on there."

"That's easy, the security guard attending the code makes a list of everyone who shows up. I'll get that right away."

Sandy closed his cell phone and felt like doing a little dance down the corridor, except his old knees wouldn't take too kindly to the workout. But he swore he would celebrate with Lenny and everyone else when the truth came out. It was just a matter of time, he was sure.

He pocketed his phone and went back to the office to ask the secretary for one more little favor.

<><><><><><>

Abrahm was mopping the floor in the repair section of the dialysis unit with a bleach solution, glancing over at Dante from time to time and waiting for an opportunity to speak to the young man. Lenny had told him how the police had made Dante one of their prime suspects, and he wanted to warn the young man that talking to Lenny was his best chance to avoid being arrested. Finally they were alone in the room.

"Oh, Dante. The police, they still look at you for killing Louie. Yes?"

Dante shrugged his shoulders. "Suppose they do. They got nothin' on me."

"I hear they do. I hear they have evidence you were in the hospital same time Louie died."

"What if I was? That don't prove nothin'. Maybe I didn't like Louie, so what? I don't kill people just 'cause I don't like them."

"But Dante, the police know you make promise to hurt him one day because Louie tell Joe West you shoot off gun in the unit. All this they have on record."

"That still can't prove I killed the fucker!"

Abrahm stepped close to the young man, reached out and touched his bare arm. "You are man with dark skin. You know the police. They not need much evidence to arrest you. And who knows what they make up, keep you in jail all your life." He urged Dante to talk to Lenny. "He is only one who can help you. I know, he help many workers in hospital. Talk to him. Please."

He handed Dante a slip of paper with Lenny's cell number on it. Dante looked at it but didn't take it, so Abrahm laid the paper down on the machine Dante was working on and went back to mopping the floor.

Out of the corner of his eye he saw the young man pick up the paper and stuff it in his shirt pocket.

FORTY-ONE

Detective Williams knocked on the door jam of the security office and stepped into the room, where he saw two rows of monitors on the wall, each one displaying a section of the hospital where a video camera was in place. Seated at the table in front of a computer with the back removed was a young man with short, curly brown hair that was already beginning to recede, a slim screwdriver in one hand and a hard drive in the other.

"Can I help you?" said the young man, turning to look at his visitor.

Williams flashed his police ID, turned and closed the door. A tall, imposing figure in his own right, Williams towered over the young man seated before him.

"You Winterbottom, the IT guy for security?"

"Uh, yeah, that's me. What can I do for you?"

"I got a problem with the video Joe West gave me. Seems it had some pieces missing. Know anything about it?"

Winterbottom put down the hard drive and the screwdriver and pushed his chair back a few inches, putting a little more space between himself and the detective.

"What's it about? What seems to be missing?"

"Two sections of the video, each one about a minute, minute and a half long."

"Well, these computers are finicky things, they're not perfect, you know. Sometimes the feed from a specific camera will fail for a few minutes. For hours, even. It's usually interference from an electronic device that's operating too close to the camera."

"Uh-huh." Williams pulled a round bar stool on wheels toward him and settled onto it. "That would be a believable story except for one thing."

"Oh? What's that?"

"The two gaps occurred right before a man was murdered up on the sixth floor. And you want to know the *really* funny thing?"

Winterbottom stared at the detective without answering.

"The funny thing is, there were no other gaps in the video for the whole night. Not for hours and hours. I know, 'cause I watched it all. The only breaks in the time stamp were right before a man was strung up by a rope."

Williams watched Winterbottom's face. The young man worked at keeping a poker face, but the tremble in his hands betrayed his fear.

Winterbottom swallowed, cleared his throat, put a hand to his face. "That's a little bit suspicious, I have to admit. I mean, it *could* be a coincidence." He saw the detective shake his head. "But on the other hand, I suppose somebody could have erased a portion of the video."

"Can you restore it? Can you locate the missing section?"

"Probably not." He saw a skeptical look on Williams' face. "The program over-writes the hard drive every seventy-two hours. The event happened a week ago. I'm sure the data is lost."

"Humor me. Check it out and let me know. Will you do that? Or do I need a subpoena and a couple of computer specialists coming in here and tearing up your department?"

"No, no, I'll run a diagnostic program right away. Tell me the exact times you're looking for and I'll see what I can do."

Williams pulled a sheet from his little notebook and handed it to the tech. As Winterbottom studied the numbers, the detective told him he'd heard the young man wanted to join the FBI.

"Yes, that's my goal. I'm taking classes at Temple on forensics and police investigation methodology. I plan on applying soon as I get my degree."

Williams stood up, held out his business card. "Call me when you finish examining the computer. If you find something, I'll show my appreciation with a call to a friend in the Bureau."

"Really? You know somebody?"

"We were in college together, played on the same team. I keep in touch with him."

"Wow, I sure will." Winterbottom took out his cell phone, snapped a picture of the detective's business card and handed it back to him. "I'm going paperless," he said.

<><><><><><>

Moose was on the fifth floor picking up late breakfast trays and menus the patients had filled out. He had a stack of union flyers in the food cart concealed between two trays laden with dirty dishes. Stopping in front of the staff lounge, he peeked in, saw an aide he knew inside and handed her several flyers.

"Give 'em out to everybody, okay Sylvie?"

"I sure will, Moose, those Croesus bastards are 'bout to run me ragged. My feet can't take it. I've been kept over mandatory overtime two times the past week. I need the money, god knows, but not if it kills my legs. How'm I gonna work without my legs?"

"Heh, heh. That's the spirit. We beat back the decertification campaign, then we go on the offensive. Instead of them writin' us up all the time, we file violations of the contract and take it to binding arbitration."

He went on to the next nursing station, seeing workers he had known for years. His feeling was, the tide was turning against the petition. The threat of the hospital going broke and closing was still scaring a lot of workers. But more and more were angry rather than frightened.

He taped a flyer to the mirror in the staff bathroom, chuckled and went on with his rounds.

<><><><><><>

"Dante, I gotta tell you, the cops have a video that shows you entering the hospital not long before Louie did the night he was killed. They know that Louie reported you for firing a gun in the dialysis unit. And they know you promised to get even one day."

The young dialysis tech had called Lenny's cell phone and agreed to meet at a fast food joint down the street from the hospital at lunch time. He scowled and cursed under his breath. "Always a woman gets you in trouble. Always a women."

"What? What's a woman got to do with it?"

"It's my girl. See, I got me a woman works the laundry four to twelve shift. Sometimes I come in at night, we find a quiet place and we have something to eat."

"Something to eat. Is that all there is to it?"

"What you talkin' about? She's got a great big bed at home, I can roll in the sheets with her any time I want. See, a lotta times I bring a little rum and pineapple juice in with me, we eat a little, we have a drink and we talk, you know? She tells me 'bout her night, I tell her about my day. It's like that."

"That sounds nice," said Lenny. "It sounds like you're serious about her."

"Yeah, I'm gonna get me a diamond ring one day soon. I know a guy. You know how it works, get it for me cheap like. But nice. A real diamond ring. Gonna surprise her one night at work."

Lenny told Dante this was great news, he could give the detective the woman's name and Dante would be in the clear. But Dante shook his head.

"No, mon, I don't giver her up. I'm no snitch, like your friend Louie. They find out she was entertaining me at work, even if they don't hear about the rum, she lose her job. Then she's in the street, we don't get married. No, I can't tell no cop about her."

"But Dante, you could go to jail. For a *long* time if you don't produce her as an alibi witness.

"My mind's made up, it ain't gonna change. I don't give her up. That's my final word."

Lenny looked at the young man, knowing he was hardheaded as well as naive about what it would be like to spend half his life in a prison cell. But this time Lenny had no smooth words to convince the young man to change his mind.

FORTY-TWO

Robert Reichart stood at the head of the conference table, his hands balled up in fists, his mouth set in a grimace.

"It seems I did not make myself sufficiently clear," he said, looking at the upturned faces watching him. "I want the union out of this facility. I want it crushed. I want it carpet bombed. And I do *not* want any of my nurses even *thinking* that joining a union, let alone the toilet bowl service workers union, will in any way help *them* or help this institution.

He told the department heads gathered at the table that if the union defeated the decertification campaign or if the nurses voted to hold a union election, he would immediately begin outsourcing some departments and privatizing others. "Laundry goes out, that will be first," he said. "I will engage a private cleaning company to provide housekeeping services."

Reichart looked around the table, estimating how many of the department heads would be gone when their departments were closed. "Billing will go to a private company and be much more efficient. Radiology reports can be outsourced to a company in India, those bastards work twenty-four seven and are grateful for the employment."

The President took out the union flyer comparing him to the Third Reich and tossed it onto the table. "West! Explain to me why you can't keep that pesky union upstart off the hospital grounds."

Joe West met Reichart's glare with cold, dead eyes. "I'll get rid of him. Give me another day, Moss won't be making any trouble after that."

"Don't screw this up, West. I'm sick of those greasy bastards defaming the good name of this institution. See that he's history."

Miss Burgess promised to fire half the nurses and replace them with new graduates if need be. "They'll be too scared to talk back to their supervisors when they realize I can replace everyone of them with an eager young nurse fresh out of school."

Reichart expressed his pleasure with her approach and encouraged the other leaders to follow her example. Then he sent them out to lay down the law among the employees.

When the meeting was over, Joe West had heard the unspoken message loud and clear. His instructions were clear; he needed no explicit words to guide his hand. Lenny Moss had to be cut down and eliminated. Firing him had only made the pest a rallying point for the misguided masses.

It was time to buy him a one way ticket to the morgue.

<><><><><><>

Seated around the dining room table, Lenny poured Moose a fresh cup of coffee from the carafe and then filled his own cup. Offering Moose the pitcher of milk, his friend said, "You know I take my coffee black and hot. The darker the brew, the better the flavor, heh, heh."

"I could give you a shot of Jack Daniels if you want to give it a little more kick," said Lenny.

Moose declined the offer, but Regis accepted, so Lenny retrieved the bottle and poured him a healthy shot.

"I wish I could join you, but I have to work down Center City tonight. A shot of Jack would put me right to sleep."

"Speakin' of sleep, how you been doing?" asked Moose.

"Uh, not *too* bad."

"Not bad?" cried Patience. "You're lucky if you get four hours of sleep a day!" She placed a tray of sandwiches on the table and poured herself a cup of tea from a little painted pot.

Moose wagged a finger at Lenny. "'Member what I told you. You're not as tough as you used t' be. That time you was sick in the hospital took something outta you. You got to pace yourself or you'll end up sick again."

Little Mary smacked Lenny in the back of the head.

"Ow!"

"Moose is right!" she said. "You got to get your rest. If'n you come into the hospital as a patient, you gonna end up down the morgue with Regis, and he be doin' *all* the talkin!"

"Christ, don't make it sound so grisly. Regis doing an autopsy on me? That *is* creepy."

"Heh, heh. Well make sure you sleep in late tomorrow. I don't wanna see your ugly face outside the hospital 'til the day shift is goin' home!"

Lenny protested that the start of the day shift was the best time to reach people. He promised to go home and sleep all day after he'd made a brief appearance in front of the main entrance.

Moose said Lenny didn't know how to have a brief appearance, but gave in to his friend. Then he reported seeing flyers about the nurses and the other workers uniting in one big union posted all over the hospital. "Fast as the bosses take 'em down, somebody puts them back up again."

"This is great, Moose. And nobody's been caught doing it?"

"No, we cool," said Mary. "We all stay away from the cameras. Ain't nobody seein' nothin'."

"What's the feeling among the workers? Are they against the decert petition?"

Regis reported most of the people he talked to were against it, especially since Lenny had been fired. "But then again, some of them are scared they'll end up out on the street like you if they keep the union."

"Some fools still swallow that shit about they can't run a lean, mean operation less'n they get rid of the union and all the if's, and's and but's that we put in our contract," said Mary. "Lean n' mean. More like dumb and dumber. I tell 'em, but some folks just don't listen."

"They're watching too much Fox news," said Regis.

"I know," said Lenny. "Did you know Canada refused to give

Fox a license to broadcast in their country? They have this old fashioned law there that news broadcasts can't release out and out lies and call them facts."

"We need a law like that down here!" said Moose.

"Ain't gonna happen," said Lenny. "But about our campaign, I think we need one more element to drive the truth home." Lenny sipped his coffee and looked around the room at is friends.

"You know," said Gary, holding half a sandwich in his hand, "if we were able to tie Louie's murder to Croesus, that would definitely sink their decertification campaign."

"It sure would," said Mimi. "I'm sure the nurses would join us, too, they'd be so angry at the complicity of management."

"Well, we can't count on anything like that," said Lenny. He explained that the lead detective on the case was investigating Dante Soleil, a dialysis tech who had a grudge against Louie, and Officer Weldon Jones, one of the security guards. "I think Louie found out that Jones and the other security guards were behind the bogus decertification committee. Louie was handing in his resignation and moving down South, so West would have no leverage on him."

"I know who Dante is," said Regis. "I bet you the cops would love to pin it on him, just for him being Jamaican."

"He actually has a very good alibi for the time Louie was killed." Lenny explained about Dante visiting his girl friend from the laundry and bringing in some rum to drink, and how the young man wouldn't give up the young woman's name for fear she'd lose her job.

"A hard head!" said Regis.

"Like someone we know?" said Lenny, raising a single eyebrow in Regis's direction. "But even if the detective found enough evidence to get an arrest warrant for Jones, it doesn't prove that Croesus was behind it."

Regis said, "If Jones killed Louie, you know Joe West ordered him to do it. And West doesn't do anything that doesn't come down from the big boss."

"I know that and Detective Williams knows that. But without proof of a conspiracy, they won't be able to arrest anyone higher up the food chain than Jones."

"We gotta get the goods on Joe West," said Mary. "That's what we need t' do."

Lenny agreed, he just didn't see where they were going to come up with the evidence. They had to rely on Detective Williams to come up with something, a plan that brought groans and protests from his friends.

"Okay, enough about Louie," said Lenny. "How do the nurses feel about joining?"

Gary Tuttle looked at Mimi, who shrugged and kept silent.

"I'd say it's fifty-fifty," said Gary. "A lot of the nurses are so fed up with the short staffing and the constant harassment, they want to join the union. But at the same time, they don't want to be in the same union as the aides and the housekeepers."

"They feel like they're professional, so they should be in a professional association," said Mimi.

"Our union is too blue collar for them," said Lenny. "I get that. Do you make it clear they would be in a separate division? They would have their own bargaining unit and their own nurses representing them negotiating their contract."

"We tell them all of that," said Mimi. "But it's an uphill climb."

"Some of the nurses want to join the California Nurses Association. Or the National Nurses United. They feel more comfortable with an all-nurses organization," said Gary.

Lenny thought if they defeated the decertification campaign, it would give the nurses the confidence to join in their organizing campaign. If the hospital collected enough signatures to call for a decertification vote, the nurses would be too intimidated to fight.

It was up to them to break the back of the anti-union drive, and for that, they had to solve Louie's murder.

FORTY-THREE

On a warm Wednesday morning Detective Williams walked up to Lenny on the sidewalk in front of the hospital and took a leaflet. "Still tilting at windmills, I see," said Williams.

"Hey, we built the windmills, we should have a say in what they do with them." He asked what was the detective doing back at James Madison.

"I want to talk to that young fellow in dialysis again, and then I'm gonna take another run at the I-T guy again in security, Winterbottom. I think he knows something he's not telling me."

"Like, security being mixed up in the drug sales?"

"I don't know. Something. He's got this dumb ass idea he's going to get into the FBI. I might be able to use that for leverage."

"An idealist! Good luck getting the truth out of him." Lenny thanked a pair of workers for taking leaflets and turned back to Williams. "You can forget about Dante, he's got a solid alibi."

"Oh, yeah? Since when?"

"Since I talked to him. He doesn't trust me too far, but he knows I'm one of the few people who can help him. It seems he's been in the habit of meeting up with a young woman works the four to twelve shift. They find a quiet spot where they can be alone."

"He's lifting her skirt, no doubt."

"Actually, he's bringing her dinner and talking about their future. He wants to marry her."

Williams took out his little notepad and asked for the girl's name. Lenny demurred. "Dante doesn't want her name given out yet, he's afraid she'll lose her job for meeting him when he's off duty."

"That's hardly a major offense."

"In this new climate with Croesus, it doesn't take much to get you canned. Anyway, Dante gave *me* her name and I talked with her. She confirmed his alibi."

"And she's solid, this woman?"

"Yup."

"Okay. At least give me the department where she works."

"Sorry, no can do. But I can assure you she'll testify for him if it comes to that. Jones is your man, I'm sure of it."

Lenny went on to tell the detective that Officer Jones was not scheduled to work at the time Louie was killed, so he had no business being in the hospital, especially in uniform. Plus, Jones was at the scene the next morning when Louie's body was found.

"I don't suppose you believe in coincidences any more than I do," said Lenny.

"Shit happens, but I'll keep it in mind."

Williams thanked Lenny for the information and walked on into the hospital, where he found Winterbottom in the security office packing up a battered old leather satchel. "Leaving so soon?" asked Williams.

Startled, the young officer snapped the satchel closed. He said he had to fix a faulty sending unit in a security camera at one of the hospital's spas in Chestnut Hill.

"I'll walk you to your car," said Williams, holding the door for his companion. They walked out past the main security desk, where an officer was giving an employee who forgot his ID a temporary day pass.

The detective waited until they had passed through the front doors and were descending the broad marble steps before broaching his topic. "Listen, I've still got a problem with the videos you gave me."

Winterbottom looked down at the ground as he walked, as if the sidewalk was littered with holes and traps.

"The stuff you gave me shows two people of interest entering the hospital around the same time as the murder victim. One of them works in your department, an Officer Weldon Jones. You know him?"

Winterbottom looked up at Williams and admitted he knew the

man, though he wasn't close to him.

"I have some good evidence Jones was involved in illegal activities, and Louis Gordon was in on it as well." They stopped at the edge of the employee parking lot. "I'm checking out some other angles, but it's looking more and more like Jones killed Gordon. So, the question I have for you is, do you want to let a killer get off, or do you want to see the guilty party punished according to the law?"

Winterbottom walked slowly toward his car, an old Honda Insight, and unlocked the door, though he made no effort to get into the vehicle.

"You've got to understand, crossing Joe West, that's suicide. I'll never get into the FBI if I do that."

"I don't know, I think you've got it upside down and inside out. I think if you help me bring this mope to justice, and I write a letter on police stationary describing how you were instrumental in bringing a killer to justice, that will go a lot farther than a letter of recommendation from a scumbag like West."

The young guard stood looking back at the hospital. He kicked a small stone at his feet. "You were right, the tape *was* altered. West doctors the videos all the time, I've seen him at the computer."

"What is he hiding?"

"I don't know exactly, it's not for me to ask. Once I caught him editing a scene with one of his guards. Jones, in fact. I always supposed they were doing something illegal."

"Like drug sales."

"That would be my first guess, yeah. When I copied the video files you asked Joe West for, I saw there were a few gaps in the time stamp. It was obvious West had been at the files."

"Can you help me? Is the missing footage really lost for good? 'Cause if the information is there somewhere and you're helping keep it from the police, that makes you an accessory after the fact. You'll end up investigated by the FBI instead of joining them."

Winterbottom swallowed hard. He looked down at the satchel in his hand and sighed. Opeing the bag, he reached down into a pocket on the inside and came up with a thumbnail drive.

"I went to the computer and copied the video soon as I heard about the dead guy on the ward. I didn't know if West had anything do to with it, but I had this bad feeling...this fear, actually, that it wasn't really a suicide. So I copied the relevant section and saved it before West had a chance to alter the hard drive."

Williams took the small device in his large hand and wrapped his fingers around it. Then he clapped Winterbottom on the shoulder, telling him he just might get into the Bureau after all, he was a good kid.

As the forlorn young guard bent low and eased into his old Honda, Williams asked him what the hell kind of car was he driving.

"It's a first generation Honda Insight. It gets fantastic mileage."

"You mean it burns gas? I thought it ran on coal or something, it's the ugliest vehicle I've ever seen."

"Beauty's in the eye of the beholder, detective. Car and Driver recorded a hundred-twenty mpg in a trip from Columbus to Detroit. Although, they were driving behind a truck with a wind barrier on the back. But hey, I get fifty on the highway all the time."

Williams had to admit, one man's ugly vehicle was a princess of a car to another. He watched as the little car pulled silently out of the parking lot. Pocketing the thumbnail, he hurried to his car where he had a laptop waiting to roll the film. On the way he called the precinct and told the officer who answered to collect the evidence from the Louis Gordon murder and check the medicinal inhaler for fingerprints. Williams had always been bothered that the inhaler was full of asthma medicine, so why hadn't it worked for the victim?

Did the killer prevent Louie from even reaching into his pocket for his treatment?

<><><><><><>

In the hospital security office, the guard at the desk saw Joe West going out and stopped him to report on the Philadelphia police detective coming back and talking to Winterbottom a second time. West asked where did they go, he didn't see them in the video room. The guard said Williams walked out with Winterbottom and headed for the main entrance.

West went back to the video room and rewound the footage for the main entrance. He watched as Williams and Winterbottom walked together down the marble steps and over to the parking lot. West switched to a view of the parking lot and saw the two standing in the lot together. Then he watched with growing alarm as Winterbottom reached into a bag and came out with a small something that he handed to the detective.

West tried freezing the frame and zooming in. The low resolution image was blurry as hell, but West didn't need a sharp picture to guess what it was. He was sure the guard who handled all his IT issues was giving the detective a copy of video footage, and the footage was almost certainly the sections West had erased from the hard drive.

Cursing softly under his breath, West put his walkie-talkie to his lips and barked, "Officer Jones, report to HQ STAT! Over."

Static filled his ear, followed by Jones saying he was in the Emergency Room and would be right there. "What's up?" Jones asked.

"Don't ask questions, just get your ass over here, *now!*"

As Jones was hurrying to the security offices, Sandy sat in his electric cart by the loading dock listening to the cryptic conversation between West and Jones. Sandy knew that Jones was West's hatchet man; that the bastard carried out any of the illegal activties that West orchestrated.

A nagging fear grew in Sandy's gut. He couldn't say for sure, but he knew that if there was one person in the whole hospital who got West's dander up, it was Lenny. And Lenny was back out at his spot on the sidewalk giving out leaflets and talking to workers as they went out for coffee or returned from lunch.

Sandy aimed his cart for the front of the hospital and silently drove around the side of the building toward the main entrance to try and find out what kind of no good deed West was cooking up this time.

FORTY-FOUR

Big and burly and pissed off, Officer Jones stood waiting for orders as Joe West closed the door to his private office.

"I've got word from the president himself. We're to silence that prick Moss. He's a threat to the hospital, he's got to be stopped."

Eager to get his hands dirty, especially with a chance to bloody a union organizer, Jones asked what was he supposed to do.

"The little bastard's out in front of the hospital again giving out his libelous literature. Go out there and arrest him."

"Okay, boss. What's the charge?"

"What difference does it make? Just put the cuffs on him and drag his ass in here. He's a hothead, he'll fight you, charge him with resisting arrest. Inciting a riot, he'll make a speech when you drag him up the steps, those types always do."

"Good, this is good"

"When you get him in the office here, *alone,* he'll have an accident. I want him unconscious, you understand? I want him bleeding into the brain. I want him ending up in the ICU with his eyes taped shut. Understand?"

"Uh, how's that gonna look, him bein' in handcuffs and getting hurt that bad?"

"No problem. Uncuff him and tell him to sit in a chair. When he does, make him hit the ground. You can say he attacked you trying to escape and you fought for your life."

"Got it."

"And be sure the bastard hits his head!"

Jones exited the office excited to have such an important assignment. It would surely mean a promotion. He might even make sergeant.

Striding quickly out of the office and passing through the main entrance, Officer Jones quickly covered the distance to the sidewalk along Germantown Ave, where Lenny was talking to a dietary worker who was talking to Lenny.

"Yo, Moss. Hand that filthy propaganda over!"

Lenny turned from his coworker, surprised. He held a flyer up in the air, saying, "What, *this?* This isn't propaganda, this is union literature, asshole."

Jones took another step forward and made a grab for the flyer. "Your shit is an attack on the hospital. You can't give it out on hospital property."

"What're you talking about? The cops already went through this, I'm on a public sidewalk."

"Bulls*hit.* The hospital property extends out to the street. Your punk ass union don't mean shit to me. I'm confiscating all your papers, hand 'em over."

As Jones made a grab at Lenny's shoulder bag, Lenny grasped the guard's wrist, trying to pry the man's fingers from the bag. Suddenly, Lenny found himself spun around. He felt one arm twisted and pulled up high behind his back. A bolt of pain shot through his shoulder as Jones pulled the arm ever higher.

"I'm taking you down, Moss. You're under arrest."

"What the fuck for?"

"For bein' ugly. For pissin' me off." He snatched a pair of handcuffs from his belt and clamped a cuff on Lenny's pinned arm. With Lenny struggling to keep his free hand out of reach, the dietary worker began running to the hospital entrance. Two men from maintenance rushed over from across the street and began yelling at Jones.

"Let 'em go! He didn't do nothin'!"

Jones ignored the onlookers as he struggled to subdue Lenny. Grabbing at Lenny's free arm, the guard wrapped his arms around Lenny and threw him to the ground. Pressing his knee into the victim's back, Jones grabbed Lenny's free arm and jammed the second cuff around the wrist. Then he heaved Lenny up onto his feet and turned him toward the entrance.

"March, dick wad," Jones snarled, pushing Lenny in front of him.

By now more workers had gathered at the scene and were yelling and crying out.

"Bastard! "

"Pig! "

"Nazi!"

"Let him go! Let him go!"

Jones pushed Lenny through the front doors and down the hall toward the security offices, while a small knot of workers gathered in the lobby wondering what they should do.

<><><><><><>

Geraldine, the dietary aide who had been talking to Lenny when Officer Jones arrested him, rushed into the kitchen and looked around the long room, searching for Moose. She peered through the steam rising from boiling pots on an old cast iron stove, but didn't see him.

"Where's Moose?" she asked Bert, one of the cooks.

"He's working the washer," the cook said, hooking a thumb in the direction of the long industrial dishwasher.

Hurrying into the washing area, Geraldine nearly slipped on the wet tile floor. She saw Moose pulling plates from the dryer at the end of the machine and stacking them on trays.

"Yo, Moose! Lenny's in trouble!"

"What? What's goin' on?" He punched the red button bringing the machine to a stop, and stepped toward her.

Geraldine explained how she had witnessed Officer Jones handcuffing Lenny and dragging him up the steps of the main entrance. Moose cursed and ripped off his apron.

"We got to get help. Go see who's in the girl's locker room and who's on break in the cafeteria. I'll get help from the hospital."

Moose pulled out his cell phone and quickly typed in a message: MEET ME AT THE LOBBY IN FIVE, WEST TOOK LENNY. He sent it to half a dozen of his friends, including Regis, Little Mary, Abrahm and Gary Tuttle. Then he went through the kitchen seeing who else he could recruit for the task.

<><><><><><>

Officer Jones pulled a battered metal chair out from a metal table and pushed down hard on Lenny's shoulders, forcing him to sit down. Lenny's hands were still cuffed behind his back. He had never felt so vulnerable, not even when he had waited to undergo major surgery.

The guard turned his back on Lenny to close and lock the door. Lenny considered charging the guy and butting him with his head, but the bastard was huge, what damage could he inflict? A move like that would hurt his own head and neck way more than it might damage the guard.

With a loud *click* the door was locked, its smoky glass window obscuring the figures in the room. Jones turned back and grinned an evil grin. A death mask smile.

"You think you're some hot shit, don't you, Moss?"

Jones reached into his pocket and came out with a roll of coins. He placed the roll in the palm of his big hand and slowly, lovingly closed his fingers around it. The fist surrounding the metal coins would deliver an extra hurt with every blow it delivered.

"You think you can just piss on the people who give you a job? Sign your pay check? Give you some place to go every day? Is that it?"

Lenny eyed the big man. He had been stuck with dirty needles at work, beaten by a murderer, even suffocated by a crazed physician. But the prospect of that fist raining down on him filled him with naked fear.

"I'm gonna see which is harder, your head or the marble floor."

Jones grabbed Lenny up by the collar and hauled him to his feet. The first blow was to the lower back right over the kidney. The blast of pain seared his flank and took Lenny's breath away. Bent over, his hands pinned behind him, Lenny looked at the wall and tried to brace himself for the next strike.

FORTY-FIVE

Reaching the lobby, Moose found a handful of workers gathered talking among themselves.

"Where'd they take Lenny?" he asked the first person he met.

"Jones dragged him down to security. They got him locked up tight, I'm sure."

"I'm goin' to get Lenny, and nobody's gonna stop me. Joe West or no Joe West, we got to get Lenny outta there before they put a hurt on him he can't take."

With calls of support, everyone followed Moose into the hospital. As they marched down the corridor, other workers they met along the way fell into line with them: a messenger from the mail room, an aide from occupational therapy, a journeyman plumber and two secretaries from the Bursar's office.

Moose walked tall, buoyed by the support of the workers behind him and confident that, whatever resistance West and his goons tried to mount, they would defeat them. It might mean they would all be fired and out in the street, maybe even in jail, but he didn't care. He and the workers marching behind him had had enough of the attacks and the cuts and the threats; the mandatory overtime and the write-ups for bullshit infractions. It was payback time.

Moose and the others reached the outer door to the security office just as Regis and Little Mary came running down the hall to join them.

"*Where he at?*" Mary called, eyes blazing. "Where's my boy?"

"He's inside," said Moose.

"Well, let's get him out!"

Moose pushed the door open and stepped in, Mary and Regis beside him, the rest of the workers crowding behind filling the doorway. A surprised young security guard was seated at a desk speaking into a microphone. His eyes grew wide when he saw the dozen or more workers crowding into the office.

"Where's Lenny?" Regis demanded.

"I don't know what you think you're doing...You can't come barging into this office asking-"

BANG!

Moose drove his fist down hard on the guard's desk, knocking over the microphone and sending a stack of papers sliding onto the floor.

"We ain't got time for no bullshit. We want to see our friend Lenny Moss right now. We wanna be sure nobody's puttin' a hurt on him. Get it?"

<><><><><><>

Lenny took a blow to the side of his head, knocking him sideways and sending him crashing into the wall. Trying to shake off the blur in his vision, he turned sideways in an attempt to discourage Jones from hitting him in the gut, his most vulnerable area, where he'd had major surgery. Twice.

Watching Jones raise his fists and consider the next place to hit, Lenny heard shouts in the corridor outside. The shouting stopped Jones, who suddenly had a puzzled look on his face.

BANG! BANG! BANG!

Three thunderous knocks on the door told Lenny only one man would be so loud and so strong.

"Open up, mother fucker!" yelled Moose.

"Who...Who says so?"

"Me and a hundred workers behind me. Open this door or so help me we'll break it down and carry your ass out of here feet first.

Jones wiped his mouth with the back of his hand, not sure of what to do. He considered calling West for instructions, but realize Lenny would overhear the conversation, which West would definitely not approve.

BANG! BANG!

"Last chance, scumbag!" called Moose.

"I got a spot on the autopsy table ready for you!" called Regis. "Got the saw and the scalpel all laid out ready to go!"

"I'm a gonna cut you up and feed you to my dogs, mother fucker!" yelled Little Mary. "Don't think I won't, you got my best boy in there!"

His shoulders drooping and face crumbling, Jones unlocked the door. He had barely enough time to step away before Moose and Regis pushed through. They grabbed Jones and slammed him against the wall. Moose had him by the throat, Regis and Mary had his arms.

"Where's the key to the cuffs?" said Moose.

"Right shirt pocket," said Jones.

Gary Tuttle, who had arrived just as the door was opening, reached for the key and quickly freed Lenny. "You okay? You want to go to the ER, I can walk you there?"

Lenny stood a moment to catch his breath. Suddenly the pain he'd been feeling vanished, the way it did for Moose in the years he was boxing in the ring.

"I think I'm okay, Tuttle, thanks. I'm not sure what to do with this dirtball. I guess-"

"I'll take over from here, Lenny."

Over the heads of the crowd of workers standing in the doorway Lenny could see Detective Williams, who had watched the scene with amusement. Williams pushed through the crowd and stood in the middle of the room.

"Detective!" said Jones. "Arrest these people! They broke into our office! They threatened to kill me! They-

"Shut the fuck up," said Williams. "The only one I'm arresting today is you, asshole."

Williams took the handcuffs from Gary and placed them on Jones's wrists, being sure they were clamped a little too tight.

"You're under arrest for the murder of Louis Gordon. You have the right, blah, blah, blah."

Williams began leading the accused out the door and down the corridor, followed by Lenny and his friends. As they reached the main lobby, Joe West came charging in, demanding to know what was going on. Williams told him he'd get a report after the DA interviewed the suspect. West tried to protest, but Williams ignored him as he pushed through to the steps and marched Jones down to the street.

Once Jones was locked in the back seat of a patrol car, Lenny asked how the detective got enough evidence to charge Jones. Williams said he'd tell him everything once the perp was booked and processed. They agreed to meet at The Cave in two hours, and Lenny promised to buy the first round.

FORTY-SIX

Sitting in the Cave over a double shot of bourbon and coke, Lenny listened closely as Detective Williams, who was drinking Jameson, neat, explained what had led to the Jones arrest.

"First off, I convinced Winterbottom to cooperate. That was crucial. I was *hoping* he had some computer-geek magic to retrieve the missing footage. Turned out the little bastard had known for a long time that some of the security guards were involved in something illegal, he claims he didn't know what, and West had a practice of altering the videos."

"But how did he find the missing data?" asked Lenny. "I thought the computer over-wrote the drive every couple of days."

"As soon as Winterbottom heard that a man had been found dead under suspicious circumstances, he copied the relevant files to a portable drive in case Joe West was going to alter them. He had them all along."

"Well, he's suspicious and resourceful," said Lenny. "Maybe he'll get into the FBI after all."

"Who knows. Anyway, I had the original video, and it showed Jones following Louie into the place where he died. Plus, it didn't show Dante Soleil anywhere near that part of the hospital."

"Son of a bitch," said Lenny. "That bastard Jones was as dumb as Louie, letting himself get caught on tape."

"Jones must have counted on West erasing the footage. Which he did. Or maybe he was just that stupid. Regardless, it was a start. I checked Louie's inhaler for prints, and what do you know, I found Jones's fingerprints on the inhaler the ME recovered from the victim's clothing."

"You thinking Jones took the inhaler away from Louie?" asked Moose.

"That's exactly what I think," said Williams. "I believe the sadistic bastard grabbed the inhaler out of Louie's hand just when he was suffering an asthma attack from the strychnine in his weed."

"Too bad you didn't find West's prints on it," said Regis. Little Mary said "Amen to that."

"The prints bought me a search warrant of the suspect's apartment, his locker at work, and his car."

"You find drugs?" asked Lenny.

"I did. Marijuana in his locker at work, oxy in his apartment, probably stolen from the hospital pharmacy."

"Yeah, but ain't you gonna arrest Joe West?" asked Moose. "He's behind all the drug sales, and Louie's murder, too! That's the whole reason he fired Lenny — to keep him from investigating the crime."

"Probably so, but Jones wouldn't give his boss up. He told the DA his dealer Weekes was behind it all. That Louie was planning on leaving town owing Weekes a lot of money, so Weeks told Jones to lean on him hard. The asthma attack was supposed to scare the crap out of Louie, not kill him. When the poor schmuck died, Jones strung him up trying to make it look like suicide."

"And we can forget about Louie's widow testifying against the security department," said Lenny. "When Matilda finally found Weekes's name on the life insurance policy, she swore she'd never say a word about it, she didn't care *who* killed him."

"You don't think Doctor Slocum was in on it?" asked Regis. "When I heard he was the one cut Louie's body down, it made me think he knew it wasn't suicide all along."

"We don't have anything on Slocum," said Williams. "But I'll keep his name on my list, you never know what evidence will shake out during a trial."

"Why stop with Slocum?" said Lenny. "He takes orders from Third Reich Reichart. That's the bastard you really want to go after."

"Now you're stretching the case too far," said Williams. "I have to go by the evidence, and the only place that goes for now is Officer Jones. And the drug dealer. West was careful not to send any emails from his personal address. He didn't send any text messages or make any phone calls from his personal phone. Everything was conducted from a prepaid cell phone."

"But you can trace the phone, can't you?" said Regis.

"It's a long shot. We'll try, but I suspect even there, West got somebody else to buy the phone for him. So there'll be no paper trail there, either."

Lenny said he'd heard West had inside information on a lot of folks working in the hospital. Stuff he uses to blackmail them into doing his dirty work. Williams said they would just have to wait and see if the fear the DA can put in Jones is greater than the one West has on him.

Moose said maybe they hadn't got West put in jail for murdering Louie, but at least they beat the decertification campaign. First Dante and the other Jamaicans took back their signatures on the petition, then half the security guards took away theirs.

"Wish I could've seen the look on West's face when he saw his own people tearing up their pledges," Moose added. "Must've pissed him off good."

"The important thing is, we won," said Bob Feltcher, who put the tab for the drinks on the union's credit card. "The nurses still haven't signed enough pledge cards to demand a union election, but they will, it's just a matter of time. And Mimi here has a little bit of job security."

He clinked his glass with Mimi's, who saw the puzzled look on the faces of her friends. "Yeah, it's really weird, but Mister Feltcher—"

"Bob."

"Bob more or less told Mother Burgess that if they messed with me, he was prepared to release a statement to the press, *and* to the state Department of Health, how Mrs. Mudge went into alcohol withdrawal that wasn't recognized, *and* how they took her to major surgery without realizing she had been taking blood thinners in the form of aspirin, because none of the doctors had taken a thorough history."

"Not to mention," said Bob, "the nursing supervisor falsified a medical document by writing in the date and time the day *after* it was actually filled out. The handwriting and the ink were totally different from the resident who filled out the consultation."

"A man after my own heart," said Lenny, toasting the union rep. Lenny turned to Sandy, who was nursing a Yeungling. "I hear you were the one who called Williams when West sent Jones out to get me."

"Guilty as charged. I heard something bad was goin' down on the walkie-talkie, so I scooted over in my cart and saw Jonesy heading toward you and I knew it was gonna be trouble. I called Williams up, told him he better get his ass down the hospital, you was in trouble."

Little Mary smacked Lenny's arm. "You wouldn't a' needed no help if you had a blade with you. Home many times've I told you, don't go out the house less's you're fully dressed!"

"I know, Mary. But carrying a concealed weapon...the possible charges, to me, it's not worth the risk."

"So pack a pair of scissors. That won't get you arrested."

As Williams smiled at Mary's remarks, admiring her savvy approach to the law, Lenny asked Moose who called him.

"Geraldine in dietary. You was talkin' with her outside the hospital. Soon as Jones started messing with you, she ran down to the kitchen and told me what was goin' down. I dropped everything and hauled ass upstairs, got to the security office with a few friends just in time.

"Hey," said Regis. "I've worked in the morgue a long time, I've seen a lot of autopsies. I don't doubt for a second West was planning on putting a major hurt on Lenny. Might even have been the kind that got you sent down to my department."

"I certainly was surprised hearing your voice. And Moose and Mary. I thought, 'what are all of them doing in security?'" He turned his head to see his wife shaking her head at him. "What?" he said.

"You dope. You still don't know how many friends you have in that damn hospital. You even have a friend in the police department!"

Lenny looked around the booth, seeing the faces, remembering the danger they had put themselves in, the meetings and the leafleting and the confrontations with the bosses, and he had to admit, he was one lucky son of a bitch.

Sandy raised his glass of Yeungling and said, "To the workers! To the union! To justice!"

"To justice!" called the rest in unison, clinking their glasses and drinking long.

FORTY-SEVEN

Bob Feltcher opened his legal pad and entered the date at the top of the page. "Lenny," Bob said, "we have a weakness and we have a strength going into the hearing today. I want your take on which one we lead with."

"Okay." Lenny had his yellow legal pad and pencil in hand and was ready to take notes. "What's our weakness?"

"The video evidence against you. It's compelling. There's no use pretending you were not away from your assigned work area for extended periods of time without permission."

"Yeah, but we do that all the time. People take an extra five here, an extra ten there, and they don't get fired for it. They might get a verbal warning, and if it keeps up, then it goes to a written warning."

"*That's* our strength. They didn't follow the step procedure in disciplining you that's spelled out in the union contract. I think we have a good shot at turning it around on that one point."

"Yeah, I was thinking the same thing. It means two weeks of back pay, too, don't forget."

"Maybe only one, the arbitrator might feel the need to throw the bosses a bone and give you a week's suspension without pay."

Lenny jotted down his notes, nodding and feeling encouraged. It was strange, being the one going on trial and being represented by somebody else, like riding in the rear passenger seat of his own car.

"Listen, I think we should bring out the real reason they fired me. The flyer calling the President 'Third Reich Reichart.' That's what this is all about. That, and fighting the decert campaign, which we *crushed* after West's goon tried to kill me."

"I understand when that young man Dante from dialysis took back his petition signature, that was a turning point for the Caribbean workers."

"And security. When *they* turned against the hospital, it was all over for Reichart and his flunkies."

Feltcher considered the issue of using the struggle against Croesus in Lenny's defense. "I'll try to get the flyer in as evidence, but the hospital lawyer will object. Since we don't have any evidence that that *was* the hospital's motivation, no emails from an administrator linking the two issues, there's no way we'll get it admitted into evidence."

Lenny wrote: NO EVIDENCE in big letters on his pad. He circled it several times, looking at the two words, and understanding this was the case he *wanted* to make. He wanted his job back, of course, but his greater desire was to show that Croesus was behind all the anti-union actions, from the decertification drive, to firing him, to all the unjustified disciplinary actions taken since the new owners took over.

Under the circled words NO EVIDENCE he wrote the name of a hospital employee who used to work at James Madison, underlined it and turned his pad around so Feltcher could read the name.

"Who's that?" asked the area rep.

"Somebody who just *might* be able to help us."

<><><><><><>

The hospital lawyer at the Step Three grievance hearing was an anorexic woman with hair dyed platinum blonde, thin lips and prominent canine teeth. When Bob Feltcher saw the lawyer come into the conference room, he leaned over to Lenny and whispered that whenever he learned Sue Ann Stapley was going to represent the hospital at a hearing he always pictured her coming into the room dressed in glossy black leather and stiletto heels.

"Kind of a dominatrix type, huh?" said Lenny.

"That's my take," said Feltcher.

Miss Stapley told the panel hearing the case that there was

nothing to even debate, the termination was an open and shut case. She presented a list of instances when Lenny was away from his assigned work area without permission. Each incident had a citation linked to a video that showed the times and places where Lenny was.

"As a union steward who is well versed in the contract, Mister Moss is all too well aware of the rules governing break times. He has exceeded them with abandon for years. His supervisor Mister Childress simply had had enough of Moss taking advantage of his position in the union and decided to apply the appropriate measure, which was termination."

Once she was seated, Feltcher rose and addressed the panel, which consisted of the acting Director of Human Resources, who chaired the panel, The Vice President for Hospital Affairs, and the Director of Patient Relations, who was supposed to bring an unbiased view of the proceedings.

Lenny's advocate said that the charges made against Lenny had nothing to do with his termination. Feltcher argued that at the time of the termination the hospital had been supporting a drive to decertify the union, and Lenny had been *associated* with a strongly worded flyer attacking Croesus, the new owner of the hospital, and the President, Robert Reichart. Feltcher slapped a copy of the flyer down on the table in front of the panelists.

Miss Stapley leapt up to object. "There is no evidence whatsoever that Mister Childress even was aware of a flyer that was critical of the hospital administration."

"The whole administration was up in arms about it. The flyer referred to the President as 'Third Reich' Reichart. It was all over the hospital."

"Be that as it may, you have no proof that that flyer had any influence on the decision to terminate Mister Moss."

"Then *why* did Joe West order his goons to employ secret police style surveillance methods, videotaping him without his knowledge?"

"Video surveillance is a legal, acceptable method for uncovering malfeasance and misconduct in an institution. James Madison has had video cameras in place throughout the hospital for years."

"But targeting a specific worker for clandestine videotaping is another step entirely. It smacks of gestapo practices. It's unAmerican." Feltcher pointed at an empty chair, saying, "And I want on the record my strongest objection that Joe West has refused to testify at this hearing."

The Patient Relations representative, who was the least tied to the administration's agenda, wanted to know what harm would come of bringing West in to answer questions. But the acting Human Resources director was satisfied that the video tapes and the summary of the incidents spoke for themselves.

"I see no point in belaboring this argument," said the chairman. "Without any credible evidence or testimony to connect Mister Moss's termination with the disputes regarding his union, I think we can move on to the concluding remarks."

Lenny glanced at Feltcher, who winked at Lenny and rose to his feet. "Mister Chairman, I call a witness to testify."

FORTY-EIGHT

Dressed in a powder blue suit, pink shirt and navy blue bowtie, Nelson Freely, formerly Director of Human Resources at James Madison Medical Center, took a seat at the conference table. Sworn to tell the truth, Freely folded his hands on the table and looked calmly at Bob Feltcher.

"Mister Freely," said Feltcher. "Thank you for coming to this hearing. You were the Director of Human Resources at the time that Mister Moss was terminated. Is that correct?"

"It is."

"Please tell us what transpired at the meeting leading up to that decision."

Miss Stapley rose on her spike heels and objected loudly. "This is hearsay evidence. We cannot allow it in this hearing!"

Feltcher reminded the panel that the rules of evidence in a grievance hearing were not as strict as in a courtroom, and that testimony regarding what an individual said or heard at a meeting specifically called about the accused was routinely admitted into evidence.

The head of the panel ruled for the union.

"Yes, I was at a meeting in which Doctor Reichart objected to the content of the flyer that the union was giving out. He was especially upset at its referring to him as 'Third Reich' Reichart."

Stapley rose again to object, but the chair silenced her with a wave of his hand.

"It was clearly stated that Doctor Reichart wanted Lenny Moss fired for his union activities, not for his occasional absences from his work area."

"Tell us more about how the security department came to videotape Mister Moss."

Stapley opened her mouth, saw the stern look on the faces of the panelists, and shut it again.

"Joe West promised to dig up enough evidence on Mister Moss by engaging in clandestine surveillance."

"Had the security department ever engaged in that type of tracking and recording an individual worker at the hospital?"

"Not to my knowledge, no, they have not. It was in my experience unprecedented. And immoral."

"You objected to the plan."

"I did, in clear and strenuous terms. But I was overruled."

By Doctor Reichart?'

"Yes, by Doctor Reichart."

Concluding his remarks, Freely turned to the hospital lawyer, who asked if it wasn't true that his employment at James Madison had been terminated for refusing to follow the direct order of his supervisor. Freely agreed, saying the order in his opinion had been immoral, illegal and beneath the dignity of the office that he held.

"But you do agree, do you not, that excessive absences from a work area without permission from your supervisor is grounds for dismissal?"

"Well, yes...And no. Not in this case."

Doing a double take, Stapley asked what did he mean.

"Well, we have a *policy* at James Madison of what is known as step-wise punishment for infractions of the rules. For infractions that do not directly threaten patient safety or the safety of other employees, we follow an escalating series of actions, the first of which is an informal counseling of the employee. Which is documented in the employee's file."

"And wasn't Mister Moss warned repeatedly about being away from his work area without authorization? He had a reputation of always wandering the halls stirring up trouble, isn't that so?"

"I wouldn't know anything about a reputation, except that he was an honorable man who helped many, many employees with personal problems that had nothing to do with the job."

The representative from Patient Relations asked Freely to elaborate. Freely told the story of the young woman in the laundry who was being beaten by her husband. Lenny brought together the laundry supervisor and the social worker to set up a mandatory inservice about spouse abuse for all of the women in the laundry. The meeting led to the young woman's first admission of her problems and, eventually, to her separating from her abusive partner.

Stapley rose to complain that the testimony was not relevant to the issue at hand. But the chair again disagreed, saying testimony about the employee's good character was most definitely relevant to the hearing.

Feltcher brought out a copy of Lenny's personnel file, asking Mister Freely if there was any documentation of informal counseling about excessive time away from his work area. Freely stated there was neither informal nor formal counseling on the subject.

"So, had you been shown the video evidence that Mister Moss had left his post without authorization, your recommendation to his supervisor, Mister Childress, would be to speak to him informally."

"That is correct."

"And if the problem did not resolve itself, you would escalate to a formal counseling."

"Yes. And if that did not solve the problem, he would be referred to me, whereupon I would probably order a three day suspension and a six month probation afterward."

"I see," said Feltcher. "But his supervisor didn't follow any of those steps that you regularly follow in cases such as this, did he?"

"No, he did not."

"And one last question, if you would, Mister Freely. Was Lenny Moss a direct, immediate threat to the safety of a patient or a fellow worker?"

"Most definitely not. He was an asset to the institution the likes of which we shall not see again for a very long time."

WIth no more questions from the hospital lawyer, Mister Freely left the meeting. Feltcher offered his concluding remarks, with

Staply providing nothing new or convincing to persuade the panel to rule in the hospital's favor.

After a half hour of deliberation in private, the chair announced their verdict. Lenny Moss's termination was to be converted to a three day suspension. He would return to work and receive retroactive pay for the time he missed, less the three suspended days.

Not entirely prepared for the victory, Lenny told Feltcher he needed a couple of days off, which the Acting Human Resources Director gladly agreed to. So long as the days were taken from his vacation bank.

When Feltcher asked what he was going to do with his days off, Lenny started to laugh. He laughed long and he laughed hard. Wiping the tears of joy from his eyes, he said he was going jogging with a friend, taking his wife out to dinner, and drinking Jack Daniels at the little bar down the street from his home until he was good and pissed, and then stumbling home and sleeping for the rest of the week. With his phone turned off and a DO NOT DISTURB sign on the door so that nobody from work could interrupt his rest.